CATO

Golden Glades Henchmen MC #7

—

Jessica Gadziala

Cover image credit: Shutterstock .com/ just dance

**"None of this book was written using AI tools.
Each word was crafted with human hands."**

Chapter One

Cato

There are some things they don't tell you are a part of being in an outlaw MC when you join up.

Like that you might be idling on your bike, waiting for one of your brothers who is having a quickie in an alley with some chick he met in a bar twenty minutes before, and he wants you to keep an eye for cops, so he doesn't land himself with an disorderly conduct charge at best, a public indecency charge at worst, the kind of thing that comes with offender registries and shit like that.

I mean, to be fair, I probably would have been in the same situation with Levee even if we never joined the club. But I'd probably be sitting inside an air-conditioned car, not sweating my ass off on a bike outside when the humidity was set to a thousand.

"For fuck's sake," I hissed, checking my watch after another ten minutes had passed.

Why not just bring the woman back to the club if you wanted to make a whole night out of it?

I mean, I got the thrill of it. If there was anyone in the club who knew a thing or two about being drawn to thrills, it was me. But this was pushing it.

I was being surly about it and I knew it. Probably just needed to get laid myself, to be honest. But I'd rather be doing that at the clubhouse in the air conditioning. Where I wouldn't be sweating all over the poor woman.

I just saw the shadow of Levee moving out of the alley, the girl in tow, when I felt it.

A whole-ass body jumping on the back of my bike, arms going around me.

"Drive!" she hissed, tone just shy of frantic.

I knew I shouldn't.

There were protocols and shit with the club, a need to check in before we got ourselves involved with anyone else's shit.

But when a woman jumps on the back of your bike, her body pressing up against yours, and asks you to get her out of Dodge, well, you fucking got her out of there. Consequences be damned.

I kicked the stand back, checked traffic, and peeled out.

Adrenaline, familiar and welcome, surged through my system, making my hairs stand on end, my pulse pound, my vision and hearing somehow become more acute.

I lived for this shit.

The edge-of-your-seat feeling when something dangerous was happening. Or even just your body's feeling of danger when you were safe.

Like bungee jumping or sky diving.

As the bike surged, the woman's thighs clenched around mine. Her arms tightened hard around my ribs, and the side of her face pressed to my back.

She had no helmet.

And I was just asking to get pulled over by staying on the main roads, but the traffic was thick in Miami on a Friday night. Even with the advantage of being on a bike that could, albeit not legally, weave in and out of the crush of cars, it was painfully slow progress to get out of the busy nightclub area.

"Faster," she called after her body momentarily loosened on mine, and she twisted to look back over her shoulder.

Someone was chasing her.

And I probably should have been kicking her off the bike. Or at the very least, insisting she tell me who it was, and what she'd done.

I didn't do either of those things, though, I just kept lane splitting, risking being pulled over and crushed between unforgiving motorists as I tried to get her further away faster.

It felt like an eternity before we finally got to a corner where I could go off to the right, into a neighborhood instead of a business district, accelerating until my stomach plummeted, telling me I was pushing it on the safety front. Especially with a passenger without something to keep her head from becoming a crushed watermelon if I made one little mistake, and we crashed.

I was considering slowing down, maybe pulling off and seeing what was going on.

But then she let out a sharp *"Fuck"* to herself before demanding of me, "Faster. You have to lose them."

A glance in my mirror said there was a car—dark, sleek, with head-splittingly bright LED headlights— was gaining on us as we barreled down the quiet street.

Now, bikes aren't great for high-speed chases.

There was more danger involved than if we were enclosed in some steel walls with some nice, puffy airbags in case of emergencies.

But they had their own benefits.

Like the fact that I could pull it down a narrow drive between houses that the car had no hope of fitting through.

It was lucky I grew up in this area of the state, knowing all the secret passageways, the roundabout ways of getting from point A to B without having to use main roads. Or any roads at all.

Like this driveway.

You wouldn't know if you hadn't spent your youth looking for places to fuck around and drink or get laid that it led into a trail meant for bicycles that all but disappeared behind a line of trees before it opened back up again to another neighborhood.

I didn't slow down on the path, wanting to put as much space between us and the car as I could before they had a chance of finding us again.

I took a left out of the neighborhood, heading away from the relative safety of Golden Glades and the clubhouse I could find there, knowing that at one point, it was a single road leading all the way out to the clubhouse, and it would be all-too easy for someone to ram into the bike, and send us flying without a single witness around.

Instead, I headed back toward my old stomping ground. The place where Levee, Seeley, and I grew up.

You know... the rougher side of town. Still run largely by rivaling gangs. One of which the guys and I used to scout for when we were kids in a bad area with parents who didn't have two pennies to rub together, so we needed to make our own money from a young age.

Besides, all we did anyway was hang around outside, none of us wanting to be a part of our living situations. So we figured we might as well get paid to do what we were already doing.

There'd been no hard feelings when we all didn't officially join the gangs as we got older. A lot of the kids who scouted didn't want to gangbang, and the gangs knew that.

Seeley had happened upon the bikers first, had been taken in thanks to his contacts that spread far and wide. Levee and I worked odd jobs until Seeley eventually tapped our shoulders to prospect for the club too.

But that extra time meant I still had a better finger on the pulse of the old neighborhood, still knew the areas it was safe and not safe to go. The places you could take your bike and hide out for a bit to let things blow over.

I drove right through one gang territory, a reasonably easy-going crew who was established enough not to worry too much about strangers on their turf, and right into a newer organization's turf. Being fresh blood in an established area, they were much more aware, more suspicious. They'd never overlook a car chase in their area, let that shit go without intervening.

I happened to have gone to school with several guys in that suspicious crew.

They knew me.

They'd let me pass.

But they'd stop anyone chasing me.

So I drove up and down those streets, pulse-pounding a lot less intensely now, knowing I wasn't getting pulled over in a place like this. Sure, cops were around. But most were in the hands of the various crews who owned the streets in these parts. They were mostly getting paid to write tickets for running reds or rolling stops. They didn't stick their noses in obvious organized crime, not wanting to fuck up their income. Or worse.

I slowed when I saw a familiar face, giving him a nod, so he knew it was me. Getting one in return, I picked it up again, but not as fast as when we were actively being chased.

Sensing the shift, the woman behind me removed her arms from my midsection, slid up to my shoulders, then thrust up into the air, letting the humid air wash over her. Her thighs clenched tighter around me to keep herself safe, and I felt an unexpected surge of desire as I heard her let out a sort of triumphant exclamation.

Enjoying that reaction, I pushed the bike just slightly faster, feeling her thighs clench again as she let out a *Wooo* as I went.

Deciding we were safe, and too fucking curious not to get a look at this woman who essentially hijacked me and included me in her crime—whatever that may have been—and forced me to become her getaway driver, I pulled the bike down an area we used to call Party Row because it was lined in several small bungalows that had been foreclosed upon decades before, and had quickly fallen to shit, and never got purchased because the crime rate in the area turned off even the most daring of investors.

Now, like it had been when we were kids, the area was used for partying and fucking and even drug deals.

Driving down familiar little front lawns, littered with glass beer bottles, handles of hard liquor, and snack food wrappers, I saw a fresh coat of graffiti on some of the houses. Big, colorful pieces of art.

There had always been a lot of fucking talent in the area. Just not the support systems to allow these artists to go to schools to hone their skills, to get them out of the neighborhood.

I pulled down to the last house, the one that had always been used the least because there were stories about it being haunted because the entire family— mom, two small kids, and the grandmother—had been murdered inside by the father who then turned the gun on himself, and no one would live there after.

I drove down the weed-filled driveway, parking the bike beside the house where it was hidden if anyone did come looking, cut the engine, reaching to pull off my helmet even as the woman behind me climbed off, stretching her legs.

I wasn't far behind, turning, not sure what I was expecting.

I think my mind had been expecting pretty. Or, at least, I wanted to attach pretty to the bare thighs that I'd seen wrapped around me.

Pretty was a weak fucking descriptor for this woman, though.

She was on the tall side with a figure that was smaller on top, and wider in the thighs and ass. She wasn't wearing much, either. Just a fucking black bathing suit top and a short black jean skirt with a frayed hem.

A skirt.

She'd been on my bike, all around me, in a fucking skirt. Nothing between us but a pair of panties.

My cock, already interested, twitched as my gaze slid over the tattoos imprinted on her arms, all black and gray, one a full sleeve, the other a mix of various things, including some sort of writing down the length of the inside of her forearm.

But I wasn't inspecting those.

Not when there was that fucking face to look at.

A round face with great cheekbones, framed in shiny, ink black hair that streamed down her back. Her eyes were edged in somewhat heavy black liner and mascara, but the eyes themselves were a bright blue.

"That was fun," she declared, smile breaking out, revealing fucking *dimples* in each of her cheeks. "Thank God you're hot," she decided, closing the distance between us, reaching up for both sides of my cut, and yanking until my body lowered toward her, then sealing her lips to mine.

Fuck the car chase.

The unexpected kiss was the most exciting part of the evening for me.

Or so I thought at the time.

Chapter Two

Rynn

What can I say?

Sometimes a girl has to jump on the back of a bike and force a man to become an accessory to her crimes.

To be fair, I had my own damn car.

Parked down a side street, unlocked, waiting for me.

But the fucking traffic was worse than I'd been expecting. And, well, I wasn't exactly planning on being caught, y'know? I'd done my due diligence. I'd planned this shit out.

Sometimes, though, it didn't matter how good you were or how much you'd planned out a job. Shit happened. You had to be willing to adapt.

I'd been tear-assing down the street, knowing that the car wasn't far behind, but was struggling to make it through the crush of traffic, when I'd seen a guy sitting on an idling bike, checking his watch, then looking toward an alley over and over.

Waiting for someone?

I didn't know.

I didn't care.

All that mattered was that he was sitting there, on a motorized vehicle that was capable of weaving in and out of the thick traffic.

I didn't stop to think. Because I'd learned that in these sorts of situations, going with your gut was the best bet.

I ran in his direction, seeing another biker and a girl pulling her club dress back into place making their way out of the alley the guy had been checking.

Rushing past them, I jumped on the back of the bike, wrapped my arms around the stranger, and told him to drive.

There was a chance, of course, that he wouldn't play along, that he would tell me to get my ass off of his bike.

But I'd lucked out that he was willing to play along, rushing into traffic, taking off into neighborhoods, then even finding some hidden trail I'd never seen before, and getting us off the main road for a while.

I figured that, once the car was a thing of the past, he would pull over, and let me off.

But he surprised me by driving me out of the party area of Miami, and into, well, the redlined area of town.

I knew the area. I'd been in the area a time or two. Enough, in fact, to know that this place was a map of different gang territories. Some more violent than others.

And this guy I was riding bitch with?

He had on a biker cut that I assumed—from his willingness to be involved with my crimes—was from an outlaw club.

So driving in this area felt risky, since his club logo said he was from the Golden Glades chapter, not

Miami.

But he didn't even hesitate as he drove around like he owned the joint. Maybe his club and this crew had some sort of understanding. Criminal organizations got chummy sometimes since allies were beneficial in a world full of people trying to take what was yours.

At some point, he pulled out of the more built-up area full of giant apartment buildings that had seen better days. You know, back in the seventies. When they were probably built. And hadn't seen an update since.

Instead, we were going down a street that seemed entirely foreclosed upon, judging by the way the grass was waist-high, littered with scattered remnants of parties and general debauchery, and the extensive and impressive graffiti art on the houses that looked all but crumbling. I imagined that if the area got hit with any sort of decently strong storm, these houses would all be gone the next day.

No one seemed to be milling around, but that didn't mean there weren't people inside the abandoned buildings. Users looking for a place to shoot up. Sex workers finding somewhere to take Johns. Or even the unhoused finding a place to stay that kept them out of the unyielding sun in the daytime. And safe from thieves at night when they were trying to rest.

I probably should have been freaking out.

This seemed like a great place to rape and murder and dump a body.

I wasn't worried, though.

I didn't get as far as I had gotten in life by being

unprepared. I wasn't packing right now because my outfit wasn't forgiving of a gun. But I had weapons on me. I always did.

The pendant necklace I had hanging down between my breasts had a hidden blade. Not huge. But in close proximity with the ability to pierce someone's neck, it could sure do the job.

There was also a reason I wore my combat boots year-round in the absolutely disgusting heat in the dead of summer in Florida. Because there were hidden compartments sewn into them—one inside the ankle, another in the tongue—where I had some other tools to do nasty things with. Plus a handcuff key. Because, well, you never knew when you might need one of those.

These were some of my favorite boots, too. Vegan leather—because, you know, the animals—a dark gray that tapered to a lighter shade and had bats all over them.

If this guy had rapey intentions, he would be in for a rude awakening.

I wasn't exactly anyone's MMA baddie, but I was scrappy. I could take care of myself.

The bike pulled to the last house on the street, parking to the side, so it wouldn't be seen by anyone coming down. At least not immediately.

The engine cut, making my ears ring a bit as I jumped off the bike, my legs feeling like they were still vibrating from the ride.

I'd been on a bike before, but I'd been the one driving it. It was an entirely different experience to ride bitch. More freeing. Probably because I didn't have to focus on driving, or worry about the other drivers always being assholes to people on bikes.

When I was sure we were safe, I'd thrown my arms up, loving the feel of the wind as it whipped me, making my hair dance all around as we rode. My stomach bottomed out at the freedom as my pulse quickened.

Every so often it was fun to do something just to feel alive. Even if that thing could also lead to your death. What was the point of living if you weren't actually *living*, y'know?

As the engine cut, though, and all those feel good emotions were still swimming through me, yeah, you could say I was feeling a bit… uninhibited.

Nothing like a life-or-death situation to kickstart your libido.

So I was just praying the biker was halfway decent looking. Enough for some kissing, maybe some heavy petting.

He felt like he was built well. With the kind of muscles that said he worked hard at his body, but not so much that he would be a complete killjoy in a conversation, only spouting out about shit like *keto* and *micros vs. macros* and *closing his loops*. You know, the guys who base their entire personality around their physique. No one liked those people.

But just because he had a slamming body didn't mean that he was kissable. Because, let's face it, faces counted more than bodies.

And voices.

I mean, no one wanted a guy to say *That's right, take that fucking cock* in a nasally, high-pitched voice. Talk about a lady-boner-killer.

But yeah, dopamine and all those feel-good hormones were racing through me as I watched him pull off the helmet, revealing light brown hair that wasn't short, but wasn't long either, and charmingly mussed from the helmet.

Then he was turning.

And, fuck yeah.

Jackpot.

The guy was smoking hot.

All the typical crap. The chiseled jaw, that kind of broody brow ridge. And, because the world was unfair and guys got things naturally that girls had to fake, he had an abundance of dark lashes around pretty green eyes.

The chances of him being that stupid hot were slim.

I felt like I found a unicorn or something as his gaze moved over me, drinking me in.

I didn't squirm, didn't try to hide the fact that I was wearing a bathing suit top like a shirt. This was Miami. It was hot. The beach was all around. Girls liked to show off their bodies. Men liked to look.

I counted on that last part in my line of work.

Sure, my titties were on the small side, but, hey, they were boobs. Guys liked those. And I would unabashedly use them as a form of distraction if I needed to on a job.

I didn't have a lot to thank my mom for, but her metabolism had served me well. And the whole way her genes made it so when I did put on weight, I did so in my thighs and ass. And thighs and asses were also popular amongst the menfolk.

I was vaguely aware of saying something about him being hot before I pounced on him.

You know… the hormones and all that.

Taking charge, I dragged him down to me, lips sealing to his.

But it was only a few seconds before he was taking over, his lips bruising into mine, his hand reaching out to grab the back of my neck, thick fingers digging in, holding me to him as his lips pressed, his teeth nipped, his tongue explored.

A soft moan escaped me as my hands left his cut and traveled up the slopes of his chest and shoulders, then down the corded brawn of his arms.

Taking his cue from me, his hands started to explore, sliding down my back to sink into my ass, fingers curling in almost to the point of pain, a sensation that sent more pleasure rushing through my bloodstream.

He used his grip on my ass to pull me more tightly against him, all my soft lines yielding to his firm ones.

His cock was pressing against my stomach, hard and yearning, making my sex clench hard at the idea of him inside of me.

Another moan escaped me, less quiet, but muffled by his lips regardless, prompting his fingers to dig in again, but this time, they slipped under the short hem of my skirt, finding nothing but cheek underneath, making me suddenly very happy that I'd recently joined the ranks of women who were comfortable in thong bikini bottoms.

His fingers were surprisingly rough, and the feel of them on my soft skin had another wave of desire moving through me, culminating in an almost painful ache between my thighs, this need for release that felt so acute that it was impossible to ignore.

The biker seemed to sense the shift, the decision being silently made, because the next thing I knew, he was moving me, slamming me hard against the house as his hand slid in between us.

His fingers pressed against the barely-there material between my thighs, and a rumbling sound moved through him.

"Fucking drenched already," he mumbled against my lips as his fingers slipped inside of my panties and teased up my cleft, finding my clit with a precision that bordered on expert, and starting to work me even as my fingers fisted in his hair, as my lips demanded more from him.

"Fuck," I hissed as two of his fingers thrust inside me, making a white-hot desire burn through me.

Then my hands weren't just grabbing his hair, they were pulling, guiding him down until he lowered to his knees in front of me, yanking my panties to the side, and working me with his mouth as his fingers kept fucking me, kept driving me up.

My leg slid over his strong shoulder as I gripped the back of his head, my hips rocking against his tongue as he worked me.

"No, stop," I said, yanking at his hair, feeling him stiffen, but pull back. And, hey, we had to dig a guy who didn't even hesitate to move away when they thought consent was being rescinded. "I need to fuck you," I said, pulling him up.

He looked a little taken aback at that.

It was always fun to catch a hot guy off-guard.

But he reached into his pocket, finding his wallet, and the condom, even as my hands were working at his button and zipper, then reaching inside to free his cock.

Long, thick. *Perfect.*

His hands brushed mine away to slip on the condom, and then he was reaching for me.

"No," I said, pulling away. "Like this," I added as I turned my back to him, hiking up my skirt around my waist.

Another of those sexy little rumbles moved through him as his hand shot out, grabbing my thong, and yanking it to my knees as he moved in behind me.

His cock slid against my pussy as his one hand grabbed the back of my neck, pushing me harder against the house with a ferocity that only managed to make me even more desperate for his cock.

Then he was shifting back, pressing against me, then surging inside.

A loud moan escaped me, despite being out in the open, as he stretched me, filling me completely.

"Fuck," my biker hissed, his fingers all but crushing the back of my neck as he settled deep, trying to find a little self-control.

I, not a praying sort of woman, sent up a prayer that he found it, that he wasn't a two-pump-chump, because every nerve ending in my body was aching for release.

He sucked in a deep breath, then on the exhale, he started to fuck me.

Hard, fast, *deep.*

His free hand dug into my hip, holding me where he wanted me as he plowed into me, making me take every inch of him with each thrust.

"Don't stop," I begged as he started to drive me up.

"Fuck, baby," he hissed in a low, savage voice right by my ear. "Feel how good you're taking me?" he asked, making my pussy clench hard around him, always a fan of a man who *communicated* when he was inside of me.

My only answer to that was another moan as he continued to fuck me relentlessly, not giving my body a second to lose the steadily-building O.

"That's it," he growled as I rocked into him as he fucked me. "You're going to come all over my cock, aren't you?" he asked as my moans got louder and more frequent, as my walls tightened, as my body threatened complete, blissful oblivion. "Aren't you?" he hissed, his fingers grabbing my hair and yanking.

"Yes," I cried, feeling on the precipice.

Then his fingers did another tug, the pain/pleasure teasing across my scalp, moving down my spine.

Then I was coming, crying out, my thighs shaking with the intensity as he pinned me to the wall, fucking me harder and faster, dragging it out, until all that was coming out of me were little mewling whimpers, the pleasure starting to ease as the orgasm subsided.

He slammed deep, growling out a curse as he came, his fingers still tangled in my hair and digging into my hip.

His forehead pressed to the back of my head after.

There was nothing but the sounds of our labored breathing and the occasional croak of a frog or chirp of a cricket.

I recovered first, wiggling enough that he stepped back, giving me space, likely thinking he was crushing me too hard against the wall. Which he had been. But I'd been oddly into it.

With the space provided, I reached down to yank my thong back into place, then pulled down my skirt before turning to face the biker who'd just managed to tuck his cock away, and was looking at me with a cocky little smirk.

"Well, that was fun," I said, smirking at him as he nodded. "Thanks for being my temporary wheelman. And the orgasm," I added. "Great job, by the way. But this is where we part ways," I told him, taking a few steps backward.

"Wait," he called, but I just kept doing my little backward getaway. "Don't I at least get to know your name?"

"I can't imagine why you would need to know that," I said, shaking my head at him.

"Let me at least drive you back to a better area."

"Aw. You don't think I can take care of myself. That's kind of cute. Misogynistic, but cute. Don't you worry your pretty little head about me. I can take care of myself."

And at that point, I was far enough away that I didn't hear what he said next. If he said anything at all.

I turned, walking right back into the bad area of town, feeling refreshed and recharged.

Was it like me to have a completely random hookup with a guy I never met?

I mean… no. Not really.

But I also wasn't going to put myself down about it.

It was what I wanted.

I wasn't going to be ashamed of a little pleasure.

Besides, I was never going to see the guy again.

So what did it matter?

Chapter Three

Cato

What the fuck just happened?

One minute, we were in a high-speed chase. The next, we were fucking up against an abandoned building.

And, God, it was really fucking *good*.

Exciting because of the adrenaline and the forbidden nature of it, sure, but it felt like more than that.

There was just something about this woman. About her vibe, about the shit she said.

Even shit like how she'd said *I need to fuck you* instead of the expected *I need you to fuck me*.

It was a very pointed difference, one that said she was fully in control of the situation. Which, of course, she was. The women always are, at the root of it. But that distinction made the whole thing feel different.

I didn't even get her fucking name.

I mean, I'm no prude. I have and always had gotten around. There was nothing wrong with two consensual people enjoying casual sex. That said, I at least learned a woman's name before I stuck my cock inside of her. Granted, no, I probably didn't remember most of those names. It seemed important, though, that I knew them at the moment.

It wasn't my dismissiveness that resulted in me not knowing her name, either. It was her choice.

Fucking wild, that was what the whole situation was.

I stood there, legs still fucking shaky from her Grade-A pussy, watching her walk away until she disappeared into the darkness.

I had no doubt that she could take care of herself, even in this area, but I felt guilty as I got back on my bike. I even drove around a bit, looking for her. Not in a creepy way. Just to offer her a ride again.

Wherever she'd gone to, though, she was nowhere in sight.

Not able to shake the sting of disappointment, I turned my bike back in the direction of the alley I'd abandoned Levee in, but he was long gone too.

One look at my phone said he headed back to the clubhouse, but that text didn't come until about five different ones asking who the woman was, where we were going, etc.

Rolling my neck, I made my way back to the clubhouse, finding it lit up with some music coming from the backyard.

Levee, it seemed, hadn't been done with his womanizing for the night. He'd probably texted the club girls on his way back home, telling them to meet him there.

There weren't many of us single guys left.

Levee, me, Alaric, and—if we counted him, which we did, albeit not officially—Eddie were all that was left. Though, from what I heard, Huck was actively looking for more prospects.

We could use that.

Because on nights like this, when I wanted to just head to bed, Levee would start shit about me being a killjoy for not wanting to party. If he had other friends to spend time with, I'd get a little more peace.

"There he is!" Levee said, standing in the pool with two girls under his arms and a beer in his hand. "Wasn't sure I'd be seeing you again tonight," he added.

"Heard you rode off with a hunnie," Eddie said, nodding his approval as he flipped something on the grill. Judging by the smell, ribs.

It didn't matter what time of the night it was, Eddie was more than willing to get some kind of food going. If you dared to suggest we just order in, he would look genuinely affronted.

"When I am standing right here?" he'd asked, shaking his head.

And, really, if you could have Eddie's food, why the fuck would you want to order in cheap, unimpressive alternatives?

"Yeah," I agreed, grabbing a beer, and popping the top off.

"Who was she?" Levee asked, untangling himself from the girls who pouted at him, then amused themselves with each other. Either from genuine interest in one another, or to entice Levee to come back and join them.

"Fuck if I know," I said, shrugging.

I didn't tell them about the car, about the chase. I couldn't tell you exactly why. I guess because I knew that would have to be reported back to Huck, then there would be questioning. And I wouldn't have answers to any of those questions.

I didn't know why she was being chased, what she might have done. What she did for a living. *What her name was.*

All I knew was what her arms felt like around me. How she smelled like a mix of coffee and chocolate. How she moaned when my cock was inside of her. How silky her hair was when it was wrapped around my hand.

None of that would be useful to Huck or the club.

Besides, I knew I was never going to see her again.

The crazy shit was, the idea of that gave me this weird, uncomfortable knot in my stomach.

"Some gorgeous chick jumped on the back of your bike, you drove off with her, and you don't know who she is?" Levee asked.

"She was gorgeous, huh?" Eddie asked, turning with sauce-covered tongs, looking between the two of us.

"Oh, man," Levee said, taking a dramatic pause to sip his beer. "Tall, long, shiny black hair, great thighs, hips, and ass, wearing nothing but a bikini top and a short skirt. And combat boots," he said, raising his brows at that one.

You can't run for your life in flip-flops.

"So, where'd you two kids go?" Eddie asked, back to flipping his ribs.

"On a ride," I said, telling the truth.

"And?" Levee asked, brows raised, anticipating.

"And nothing. That's it."

I didn't lie to Levee. We'd been best friends since

we were kids. We'd grown even tighter when Seeley had left our crew to join the bikers. We knew all the good and bad about each other. There was no reason not to tell the truth.

But I dunno.

I guess I just wanted to keep it to myself.

"Oh, come o—" Levee started, breaking off on the sound of a car horn beeping out front.

We didn't have any neighbors.

"More club girls?" I asked as Levee shook his head, suddenly sober, and ready for anything.

"Girls, stay here," he told them. "Keep an eye on 'em," he added to Eddie, getting a nod as I reached for my gun, and he went to fetch his own.

Then we moved around the house, pulses pounding, ready for just about anything.

"Christ," I hissed at the sight of the very familiar car.

Riff and Raff were dropping in for a visit.

Riff and Raff, twin brothers from our sister chapter in Shady Valley. They were kind of nomads, spending most of their time driving around the South, hitting up gun shows, buying shit that would never trace back to them or the club, and driving the illegal guns back to California to be shipped out to clients.

The thing was, our business had really started taking off in Golden Glades ever since we made a deal with Zayn, an international arms dealer, who had clients all over the world. Ones who paid a pretty penny for the guns we could supply.

The problem was, we couldn't find enough guns from our usual sources to keep up with Zayn's contacts' needs.

Enter Riff and Raff.

Who were willing to supply to us, for a cut to the Shady Valley crew.

The car pulled inside, and I'd seen it several times now, knowing that the panels inside pulled out, so guns could be stored inside. Same for the floors and even some of the seats.

Riff and Raff climbed out a second later.

The family resemblance was obvious.

Both men were tall and fit, dark-haired, dark-eyed, with square jaws. The differences were subtle. Riff, the older brother by a few minutes, had a sort of cultured stubble and one arm sleeve. Raff was clean shaven, but was completely covered in ink.

They were dissimilar in personality, too. Riff was a bit more standoffish, more serious. Raff was out there and wild, always down for a good time. Which was what they were probably looking for.

"Weren't expecting you," I said, shaking Riff's hand.

"We're between shows and meet-ups," he said. "Hanging here sounded better than another hotel."

"Well, good timing!" Levee said, always happy for more people to party with. "We got some pretty girls. Beers are cold. Eddie has ribs on the grill…"

The party was still going strong when I made my way inside, tucking Mackie—the club's blue and gold macaw—into his cage for the night, so he didn't get into any sort of trouble.

"*Fuck you*, Benny," he grumbled with a lot more vitriol than usual, likely pissed that his plans for trouble were thwarted for the night.

"Yeah, yeah, yeah," I said, turning the light lower, so he could hopefully get some sleep, even with the party raging outside.

"Christ, you're getting in late," I said as Alaric came in through the front door, carrying his usual gym bag.

"Had to hit the gym."

If anything, Alaric needed to lay off the gym. He'd been getting skinnier than ever lately. Enough so that some of the guys had even tried to talk to him about a possible eating disorder. It... hadn't gone well.

Now, he was just working out 24/7.

I mean, I worked out a lot. I liked to keep definition, keep up my strength. And I was always trying different shit. I'd recently picked up indoor rock climbing, something that worked damn near every muscle group, and especially grip strength.

But I understood that there was a fine balance between taking care of your body, and even taking pride in it, and being obsessed with it.

Alaric was obsessed.

Something we all surmised maybe stemmed from his years exotic dancing, when his income and identity depended on how good he looked.

I could see how that kind of thing could warp your view of yourself. Especially after the job ended, and you suddenly weren't getting praised over your looks all the time.

"Eddie is cooking," I told him. "Riff and Raff are crashing," I added.

To that, he nodded, but made his way upstairs

before me instead of going out to be social.

Shaking my head, I made my way to my room as well, grabbing some clothes, and making my way to the bathroom.

Some part of me didn't want to shower, to wash the chocolate and coffee scent of the random woman off of me. But that was so insane, I made myself get under the cool spray, and scrub body wash over me.

The last thing I needed to do was to get sentimental over some random chick I was never going to see again.

Chapter Four

Rynn

"Rynn!" Josie, my best friend slash employee slash right-hand-girl slash my voice of reason hissed as I sat in front of her desk, legs kicked up on the edge, sipping a much-needed Big Gulp of soda. One of my —admittedly, many—vices.

"Oh, come on. Fucking a guy against an abandoned building is hardly even the most shocking thing I have ever done." I mean, were we forgetting that time I went streaking through a casino to draw the cameras and security guys in my direction so they never suspected why I had really been in their establishment? Men tended to lose all their common sense at the sight of a little T&A.

"You don't even know his name!" Josie insisted.

Josie was the antithesis to me.

Where I was tall and bottom-heavy, she was short and sporting a rack men would cry over and dedicate sonnets to. Where I was dark-haired and allergic to all things color, she was a strawberry blonde who loved bright, feminine shades. Where I was often uninhibited, brash, and bold, she was straight-laced, shy, and careful.

We made a great team.

But I was ninety percent sure that if she started to

go gray before the appropriate age, every single silver strand would be thanks to me.

That was what I brought to a friendship.

Stress.

But a fuckton of fun stories.

And the absolute best places to eat and drink.

Not that Josie indulged much in booze, but when she did occasionally let loose over bottomless cherry-lime margs and chips and salsa, she always enjoyed some story of my antics from before her time.

She'd only come into my life two years before. And let's just say that there was a lot of debauchery in the years prior to that.

It was hard to believe it had been such a short partnership. I didn't know how the hell I'd functioned without her in my life.

Josie was the much-needed tether that kept me from being swept away with any random bad idea.

"Yeah, that was a little unlike me," I admitted.

I mean, no. I wasn't someone who held themselves back from enjoying adult glandular-to-glandular contact. I had no shame when it came to my sexuality. That said, yeah, I did always know the *names* of my partners. In fact, because I was busy and didn't have a lot of patience with finding partners, I usually ended up having friends-with-benefits situations. I had two previous boyfriends that I always go back to when I needed a quick tour of the sheets. It made life easier that way.

"Did he catch your name?" Josie asked, still hung up on the name thing.

"No," I admitted. "He did ask," I clarified.

"And you didn't tell him?"

"Josie, I jumped on his bike and implicated him in my crime," I reminded her. "The last thing I need is for him to actually know who I am, and have him coming around and asking questions."

"I guess that's true," she agreed, looking a little crestfallen.

Josie was of the hopeless romantic class of people.

She cried over rom-coms and those really dramatic, drawn-out-over-ten-seasons love stories on TV. She always had a romance novel in her top desk drawer since her job didn't require a lot of her during the day.

I knew that she had her heart set on a happily-ever-after of her own. And, because she loved me, one for me as well.

Even if I was decidedly less romantic.

I mean, don't get me wrong. I had some love stories I enjoyed. Gomez and Morticia were couple goals if I'd ever seen them. But I'd just… never been in love, y'know? And if you reach the old age of twenty-six without ever being in love—even young, puppy love as a teen—you start to question if it really exists at all, or if it was just something novelists, producers, and poets all made up out of some sincere wish that it were real.

So, yeah, I wasn't planning on some man to sweep me off my feet.

And my version of a happily-ever-after was me on the balcony of my penthouse with a margarita in my hand, watching the sunset after a long day of doing something mildly crazy, and not having to work anymore.

Don't get me wrong, I enjoyed my job. I just didn't want to do it forever. And since a lot of what I did relied on using my physical appearance as bait or a distraction, I understood that there was a clock on how long I could do it anyway. I figured I had until my mid-thirties to build my nest egg.

I mean, sure, I planned to be a banging hot old lady in the nursing home, but let's face it... guys are nothing if not predictable. The second they spotted a set of crow's feet, they were looking for someone more perky and bouncy and not at you anymore.

This meant that the clock was ticking, and I was busting ass these days to make every minute of it count.

Hence, the shitshow that was the job the night before.

Were I still twenty years old with all the time in the world ahead of me, I wouldn't have taken one on such short notice with the small amount of planning I had. But I was trying not to turn away good money when a job did fall in my lap.

My job was pretty in-demand, since not many people thought to open up a practice like mine, but that didn't mean that I had clients coming out of my ears every day.

I used to be okay with doing some thumb-twiddling between clients, but now I just wanted as full a calendar as possible.

I mean, sure, I had a nice apartment. And I even had a good savings going. Even if I invested that money wisely, though, I doubted my ability to make it until my timely death at one-hundred-and-one years old, after just having given an interview to the local news station telling them that tequila, coffee, soda, and junk food were the secret to my longevity, with just what I had stored away now.

And I didn't want to struggle, to pinch pennies and cut coupons. I wanted a long and easy retirement from the age of thirty-five on. Which meant hustling hard now.

"That was too close of a call last night," I admitted to Josie. Since she was the only person I ever confessed that sort of thing to.

"Yeah, it sounds like it could have ended really badly."

It could have.

I'd been lucky.

I mean, to be fair, I was skilled and adaptive, so I would have found another way if the biker hadn't just been sitting there like an open invitation to hop on.

But it would have been harder to get away under a different circumstance. I'd have managed, but still.

It was too close.

I had to be smarter.

"You know, I could—" Josie started to offer.

"Absolutely not," I cut her off, knowing what she was going to offer to do. Be a wheelman for me on iffy jobs.

But this was *Josie* we were talking about here. The girl who had a granny tap on her accelerator. The one who signaled way ahead of her turns. Who allowed everyone to cut into traffic ahead of her. She was careful and courteous. Which was great for society, but shit for a wheelman.

"You are my office princess, and I refuse to have it any other way."

"There's almost never anything to do here," she insisted, waving around the empty space.

I had an official office space.

I had a registered business name.

Black Cat Consulting.

Named, of course, after my love of all things Halloweeny. Including my three black dumpster cats. One of whom was our office mascot since he hated his siblings back at home. Josie took Binx home with her most nights, but he was just as happy to stay in the office, and would sometimes scratch the shit out of her when she tried to grab him and put him in the crate to leave.

The office itself was on a strip that featured several other small businesses. A dentist, an eye doctor, a shoe store, and a nail salon.

It wasn't a huge space, but it was more than big enough to feature a desk for Josie, a couple of seats on the other side of it, a couch near the back for me since I wasn't a desk sort of chick, and a bathroom to the right, and a tiny kitchenette/break room to the left.

More than enough for our needs.

Since, like Josie said, we weren't exactly a busy office.

But we had to keep up appearances.

Taxes and all that crap.

The picture window had mirrored film on it, so we could see out, but no one could see in. But it also allowed in a teensy bit of light without letting the place bake when the sun was beating on the strip.

I didn't want anyone knowing our business. And I also didn't like anyone being able to notice that Josie was alone in the office most of the time. It was also why I insisted she keep a taser in her desk, just in case.

I'd decorated the inside of the office to suit my personal tastes. To hell with the clients.

The walls were a slate gray, save for the one brick wall across from Josie's desk. Her desk itself was intricately carved and antique. The chair I was perched in—and the one beside it—was a royal high-back velvet chair in a deep, blood-red shade.

In the back, the couch was a black tufted thing with antique end tables. One had a golden human skeleton lamp; the other was a big raven lamp.

Every one of Josie's desk supplies were in bright colors, putting a bit of herself in the office that in no way suited her tastes. Neon pink sticky notes. A baby blue pen holder. A canary yellow notebook. Even her coffee cup was a floral print in shades of purple, pink, and blue.

Hell, even Josie herself stood out in the goth-chic look of the office. From her nearly one-hundred-percent Irish heritage, she was almost ghostly pale with some charming freckles. Today, she had another of her sundresses on, which she practically lived in, because she claimed '*They're effortless, but make it look like you are all done up.*' This one was a light blue with white flowers which only made her deep blue eyes pop.

She was so freaking pretty.

I'd put good money on her being able to find that happily-ever-after of hers if she would just... leave the house once in a while.

"Tell me again how pretty he was," she implored, giving me a girlish smile.

I was pretty sure that neither of us had ever had close girlfriends before. Me, because, well, my whole all-halloween-all-the-time and rough-around-the-edges personality just didn't fit in with the cliques in my schools. Josie, because she apparently went through an extremely painfully awkward stage. Headgear and all. That, paired with her innate shyness, and it seemed like she was just as on her own as I'd been growing up.

So after we'd gotten over the initial awkward phase, she and I had started to cling to each other the way teen girls do. Like a lifeline. Sharing all the details about our lives.

She knew how my cherry got popped on the hood of my ex-boyfriend's brother's car in an act of revenge for being cheated on.

I knew that she'd held onto her v-card until the morning before her twenty-second birthday, and that she'd done it out of desperation with her neighbor across the hall who was a world-renowned manwhore who she knew would fuck her in a heartbeat. *My words, not hers.*

Unfortunately for her, the dude got all weird afterward when he realized she was a virgin, and did everything in his power to avoid her in the halls and parking lot since.

That had been going on for a year.

Which probably gave the poor girl a complex about it.

Honestly, I didn't think she'd been with anyone since, but I didn't press about it. I could see that being a sore spot after such an awkward first encounter.

Sure, my initiation into sex had been for revenge, but I'd made the right decision by giving it to the older brother who actually knew what he was doing and gave me a good O before the actual act. Not too shabby for a first time.

She lived vicariously through her romance smutty scenes and my very detailed accounts of my own sexcapades.

"Oh, God, Josie, he was so fucking pretty," I said, letting out a little sigh at the memory of him, then taking a long sip of my soda until it slurped and I sucked in a ninety-percent water mix that had my nose wrinkling.

"Green eyes, you said, right?" she asked, smiling wistfully.

"Gorgeous green eyes. And when they're looking at you like a meal he wants to eat?" I said, letting out a dramatic sigh. "It's a shame he had to be a one-and-done, because I could have turned that into a couple-month-long royal fuckathon, and been a blissfully happy woman."

"Hey, maybe you will run into him again one day!" she said, ever the optimist. And you had to love her for it. Even if Miami was home to almost half a million people. The chances of running into your neighbor on the street were slim, let alone some dude you fucked once.

The statistics were wholly against it.

Still, though, it seemed Josie's wish would come

true just a few days later.

Chapter Five

Cato

"Eddie, we could have just picked up some hot dogs or something," Riff insisted as Eddie came walking toward us on the beach, dragging a giant-ass cooler behind him.

He was in a pair of green board shorts with a yellow and white bowling shirt on top, shades, and flip-flops that kicked sand up with each step.

Levee and the guys had followed the club girls to the beach. Then we'd stayed after they headed back home because, well, the beach was full of other chicks.

Levee and Raff were off playing volleyball with some of them right now. Alaric was taking a run beside a woman doing the same, the two of them striking up a conversation as they went.

Leaving just me and Riff with all our shit.

Me, because I was uncharacteristically disinterested in spending my time chasing women. And Raff because he likely felt bad leaving me alone.

"Beach cart hot dogs?" Eddie asked, looking downright offended. "Not on my watch. I got homemade subs, wraps, and sandwiches. Cole slaw, pickles, chips, everything we could need," he told us as he flipped the lid open.

"Why are there so many sunblock tubes in here?" Riff asked, brows pinching.

"'Cause they're not sunblock," he said with a smirk.

They were Eddie's special liquor-hiding system.

"But if the cops ask, we're just super concerned about skin cancer, man," Eddie added, hunkering down, and grabbing himself a sandwich. "So, what's the plan for tonight? Clubs then crashing at Teddy's?"

"Probably," I agreed, admitting that it was really out of my control. This was Levee and Raff's party. We were all just tagging along. "But we have to be home early tomorrow," I added, reaching for a sandwich too.

"What for?" Eddie asked as he squeezed clear 'sunblock' into the soda he'd taken a chug out of to make room.

"Prospects," I told him.

"Been a while," Eddie said, looking at me.

And that was true. Levee and I were the newest members of the chapter, and we'd been around for a long time.

"OG guys have been busy building families," I said, shrugging.

"It'll be good. We could use some new blood around here."

We all had to agree with that. All things considered, we had a small club, given how long we'd been around now. Nothing like our mother chapter, of course, that had been around for generations. But the crew in Shady Valley was growing at a much faster rate.

Granted, they lucked out that their clubhouse is near a prison, and they can recruit new members from the inmates being released.

But we had close enough proximity to Miami, and the crime going down there, to be able to find new brothers too. It just hadn't been a priority until business started picking up.

Now, we needed fresh blood and quickly.

It was the first time the club had ever had a sort of recruiting process. Huck, Che, McCoy, and Remy all knew and worked together before the club formed. Seeley had been at the right place at the right time and proved his worth. He brought Levee and me in. Che brought in Donovan and Alaric through old contacts. And Eddie, though he wasn't officially a club member.

This would be the first time that men would be joining up without some prior involvement with the club or its members.

Shit would be interesting.

And I had a feeling the club was going to be hopping more often than it wasn't with some new guys around.

Normally, that would have at least had some appeal to me. But I found over the past couple of days, that I was just not feeling the partying vibes Levee and Raff were creating.

I'm sure if I tried hard enough, I could convince myself that it was just a funk, that I needed to shake things up, find some new, crazy hobby to get the adrenaline going, and then I'd feel right again.

Thing was, I wasn't trying to find some bullshit excuse. I knew what the problem was.

A fucking knockout of a woman had swirled into my life, a tornado that had sucked me up, then spat me back out in a different place, and I was feeling a little fucking off about it still.

Crazy?

Sure.

But I wasn't going to try to blame anything else for the weird headspace I was in.

I mean, last night, Levee and Raff had no less than half a dozen girls playing strip poker in the backyard, and I'd just walked by, grabbed a beer, and went up to bed.

Without even stopping to think how fucking weird that was.

Even now, on the beach, I could be watching the chicks playing volleyball in bikinis, bodies jiggling in all sorts of interesting ways. But my gaze was scanning the beach and boardwalk instead, wondering if there was a chance I could catch sight of that long, gleaming black hair, those tattoos, that gorgeous face with the fucking dimples.

But she was nowhere.

Of course she wasn't there.

First of all, the chick was pale. Not the kind of woman to be lying out on the beach.

Second, it was a big fucking town. The odds of seeing her again on the rare occasion we were in Miami were low.

I needed to get a fucking grip.

That was why I agreed to hit the town after the sun went down and the guys weren't ready to go home.

I wanted to get my head off of the random woman, and back in my current life.

"My friends!" a familiar voice called as we were

getting in line for one of the many clubs on the strip.

Turning, we found the man himself, Zayn, our international arms dealer, sliding out of the passenger seat of a white Pagani Huayra with a black and red interior, its gull-wing doors up, and drawing looks from everyone around.

Including Eddie.

"Man, that's a cool one-point-five mill for that baby," he said, a gleam in his eye as he looked at it.

Zayn was already out, leaving his right-hand-man Daniyal in the driver's seat, waiting to make sure he didn't want to get back in.

Zayn was tall and slim, but fit, under his perfectly tailored short-sleeved dress shirt and slacks. He had black hair, a black, neat beard, golden skin, unknown heritage, and warm brown eyes.

"Hey, Zayn," Levee greeted, moving away from the line to do the whole handshake / one-armed hug thing.

"You weren't about to get in *line* for the club, were you?" he asked, sounding horrified at the very idea.

"We heard good things about it," Levee said, shrugging.

"Things worth not waiting for," Zayn said, waving at the rest of us to approach as he walked to the bouncer, shook his hand, and was let right in, with all of us in tow.

"Eddie, you coming?" I asked, seeing him still eye-fucking the car.

"Think he'd give me a ride, man?" he asked instead, looking at Daniyal.

"Probably."

"Gonna shoot my shot," he declared, walking in that direction, ducking into a squat to be seen under the fancy-ass doors.

Then Daniyal was shrugging, Eddie was slipping inside, and they were gone.

The bouncer was giving me a look, so I made my way into the club, trying to ignore the urge to just... call up Teddy, ask him if I could crash at his place early instead of doing this.

But that urge was exactly why I kept putting one foot in front of the other until I was swallowed up by the club.

Now, clubs were clubs. Generally speaking, if you've seen one, you've seen 'em all.

Long bar. Dark lighting with the occasional neon accent or strobe. Music so loud it pulsed into your feet and through your whole body.

But I had to admit there was just... something different about this one as Zayn led us up to the VIP section like they saved a table just for him, on the off-chance he wanted to drop in on any random night of the week.

The crazy shit was... they seemed to.

The hostess gave him a big smile, and immediately reached for the special menus for the section. "You know where your table is, Zayn," she said.

And, apparently, he did.

The biggest one right in the center of the section. It even had a "Reserved" sign on it.

"Do you just... keep this reserved all the time?" Riff asked as we all got seated.

"For the past few months. I never know when I

44

may want to drop in. And life is too short not to have bottle service from our very own server."

"What does she do when you don't show up, then?" Riff asked.

"Enjoys getting paid to do nothing?" Zayn suggested.

"Do I even want to know what this sets you back?" Levee asked, never afraid to ask the inappropriate questions.

"It is not… insignificant," Zayn admitted.

But this man paid over a million for a car. And I suspected it was only one of several he owned. So our ideas of significant and insignificant amounts probably didn't exactly match up.

It wasn't long after we were seated that our server —a pretty blonde who asked Zayn how his sanctuary was coming along—was bringing us champagne, and taking orders for more.

"Sanctuary?" I asked.

We weren't exactly close with Zayn.

He was elusive. Always breezing in and out of town. When he was around, he was down for a good time, but it was always light and superficial. Drinks, food, girls. Then he was gone.

We rarely got a chance to actually get to know the man. Aside from hearing his stories about traipsing around the world. And the occasional account of some near-death high-speed chase or near-miss hostage situation.

It never ceased to amaze me that a man as notorious as he, one who had the kind of money he clearly had, didn't have an entire crew of personal security around him.

He had Daniyal.

A man who had fucked up his own fingerprints.

One whose gaze was always moving around a room.

Some sort of ex special forces.

Clearly trained enough to get his boss out of damn near any situation in all different countries around the world.

"Yes, I am in the process of opening a sanctuary," Zayn said, nodding.

"An animal sanctuary?" Levee clarified.

"No, my friend. One for old sports cars, so they can live out their golden years in peace," Zayn said with a smirk. "Yes, of course, for animals. Ladies!" he said, waving a crew of gorgeous, scantily-clad women up into the VIP section.

There was no more getting personal information out of him. He was in party-mode.

It wasn't long before the others were as well.

Sometime within an hour later, Daniyal was leading Eddie through the crush of bodies, his keen eyes looking around the club like there might be enemies hidden in plain sight.

And, I guess, in their line of business, there might be.

He sat there at the edge of the table, watching the club, sipping on a lemon-lime soda, as his employer and my brothers yucked it up.

I'd been babying a beer for the better part of half an hour when it happened.

A whip of shiny black hair.

Granted, it was a club. Hair was whipping everywhere. Of every different shade.

But there was something in my stomach that jerked at the sight. And I swear, even across a crowded bar full of headache-inducing cologne and perfume, I could smell that chocolate and coffee scent that clung to those strands and her body as a whole.

But the bodies were moving, a big mass of undulating dance movements, making it hard to pick any singular person out when the occasional light flashed over the crowd.

I kept my eyes peeled on the place I thought I'd seen her. But when the light flashed again, the woman was several yards in the other direction, walking swiftly toward the door.

Almost like she was on the run again.

But from what?

From who?

It made no sense.

As the light flashed again, though, I saw the black and gray tattoos on her arms, and I knew.

It was her.

I was up and out of my seat before the thought even formed. Out of VIP, then the club, before anyone could even think to ask me where I was going.

I had no idea.

Wherever *she* was going, that was where.

It was hard to find her at first as I moved outside, finding myself oddly disoriented from the light and lack of noise.

My head was on a swivel for a solid minute before I caught that hair kicking up on the slight breeze.

From the other side of the street.

I charged out into traffic, just narrowly avoiding getting swiped by a passing SUV with a bikini-clad woman *woo-hooing* out of the open sunroof.

She was tall, but her pace was more than just being long-legged. It was hurried, without looking like she was trying to run away from something or someone. She had that purposeful urgency of a woman walking alone at night, that 'don't even fucking think about it' gait and posture.

She left the main drag, going down a side street, then cutting down another street so quickly that I almost missed the turn.

I was being creepy as fuck.

I was aware of that fact.

But I couldn't seem to make myself turn away, go back to the club, forget about this woman who clearly didn't want to see me again if she refused to give me her name.

I almost missed her.

Again, it was the hair I saw.

Disappearing into a storefront on a small strip with all darkened establishments.

Honestly, I was so focused that I didn't even pay attention to where I was, what the other businesses were, or even what the one she went into was. One that was open way too fucking late at night.

I was about to knock on the door.

Then it burst open, a hand shot out, grabbed my shirt, and dragged me in.

"You're really fucking creepy, you know that?" she asked as she slammed me back against the door.

"Yeah, I—" I started, searching for any sort of excuse for my behavior.

"And also a shitty, shitty trail," she added, pinning me with those blue eyes of hers. "It's lucky you're hot," she added.

Then her lips were on mine.

Hard, demanding.

And I had no choice but to follow her lead.

As if I wanted to do anything else.

Her body plastered to mine as her arms wrapped around my neck.

My own hands were restless, going down, sinking into her ass, squeezing, then pulling up.

Until she was on her tiptoes.

Then not making contact with the floor at all.

Hooking her arms more tightly around my neck, she pulled her legs up my sides until they wrapped around my lower back.

She pulled back just long enough to say the one thing I really fucking wanted to hear right then.

"Couch," she demanded.

One quick glance past her showed the shadowy outline of one in the back. Next to a golden human skeleton lamp that was giving the dark room its only light.

Grabbing her ass more firmly, I held her against me as I walked toward the couch, turning, and dropping my ass onto the cushions with her straddling me.

The second we were seated, her lips were ripping from mine, going to my neck as her hips ground down on my hard cock, making me let out an almost pained groan.

Then she was moving, sliding off of my lap and onto the floor, her hands dancing up my thighs, then coaxing in, working my button and zipper free, then sliding her hand inside to pull out my straining cock.

Reaching out, I grabbed her hair, getting it out of the way, and wrapping it around my hand as she lowered down, as my cock slid into her warm, wet mouth.

My hips bucked up into her mouth at the sudden sensation, but she was taking over fast, sucking me fast and deep, over and over, doing little twists, her hand cupping my balls.

I could have let her keep going.

But then my hand was pulling, yanking her back by her hair until my cock left her mouth.

I'd been fantasizing about being inside of her again since the moment she'd walked away from me.

I wasn't going to miss out on the opportunity to have it finally happen again.

Taking my cue, she moved away, her soft hair slipping over my hand as she moved to stand in front of me.

Her hands slid under her skirt—another short, black number, but this one a tighter material, not a cut off jean type—and snagged her panties, pulling them slowly down, a swatch of black material slipping down her long legs, before she was stepping out of them entirely.

I reached into my pocket for my wallet, then the condom, slipping it on.

Then she was moving over me again…

Chapter Six

Rynn

I'd been on a job in the club.

That's not to say that I don't enjoy the occasional drunken night dancing. But I typically chose to do that while dragging Josie with me, both of us letting our hair down, and enjoying each other, trying to ignore all the dudes who were just looking for a fuck.

I didn't go to clubs alone for obvious reasons.

Except, of course, when I wasn't drinking, when I was focusing on the work itself.

Sure, I made myself seem stumbling and uninhibited. It went with the cover. But I was actually laser-focused, and getting shit done.

It was an easy job, all things said.

One hour of work.

Quick five grand.

Not exactly 'rolling in it' money, but, hey, who would turn down five grand for an hour of their life?

Not me.

That was money for the nest egg.

I was just about finished with the job when I felt it. That prickly feeling on the back of my neck. That absolute certainty that someone was watching me.

It was a skill most women learned early, being acutely aware of predators all around. It was one I'd honed even more as I started working in a, let's say…

less than reputable sort of business. One that could literally mean life or death if I took the wrong job and got caught doing it.

So I felt the eyes.

Then, as I moved outside, I felt the presence behind me.

But, again, I wasn't a damn idiot.

I deliberately walked past storefronts with plate glass windows, sliding my gaze to the side to watch the reflections as we moved.

It wasn't easy work.

We were hardly more than shadows.

But the details became more apparent as we kept walking. The tall, wide frame. The defined facial features. The jeans, tee, and then, finally, the leather cut.

This was my biker.

The guy I couldn't stop thinking about fucking again since I'd walked away from him. The one I was sure I'd never seen again.

I wasn't like Josie.

I didn't believe in the stars aligning and shit being meant to be. But I did believe that sometimes life could toss a fun coincidence at you.

And I was all about grabbing those little opportunities when they came at me.

So I led him down the strip, then a side street, then finally onto the street with my little business strip.

Stupid? Maybe. It meant he would have a way to find me again.

But I was too high on anticipation to force myself to make a better decision.

I just rushed ahead, unlocking my door, then disappearing inside.

Where I lay in wait for him to come by.

Then grabbing him, pulling him inside, and all but jumping on him.

Desire was a spark that ignited into a wildfire that raged through every inch of me as my hands were on his, and his on mine.

The ache between my thighs was painful as he took me back to the couch, sat down, and had me straddling him.

Some part of me wanted to take our time, explore, at least get some clothes off this time. But the need was too acute to deny.

There was almost no foreplay, save for me sucking his cock for a couple short minutes.

Not that I needed it.

I was dripping wet already.

I watched him slip on the condom as I pulled off my panties.

Then I was climbing over him, feeling his cock press against my pussy as my lips sealed to his once again.

I rocked against his length, engaging my clit, as he took over the kiss. Deepening it. Tongue teasing. Teeth nipping.

His hands were on my bare ass, using it to drag me more roughly across him, my little whimpers getting swallowed up by his lips.

Then, impatient, I was reaching between us, grabbing his cock, and holding it as I lifted up, as I positioned over him, then lowered down, feeling his cock slip inside of me, inch by delicious thick inch, until he was settled deep.

"Fuck, you feel good," he growled against my lips, making my walls tighten around him.

I had to concur.

He felt fucking amazing.

Better, even, than I'd been fantasizing about in bed with my stupid vibrator that just wasn't cutting it. Not when what I wanted was a real, flesh-and-blood man. This one, in particular.

The biker's hands went down to my ass again, one hand sinking into a cheek, the other one giving the other a hard slap.

"Fucking ride me, baby," he demanded, making my pussy do another little squeeze. At the pain/pleasure of his slap, but also the little endearment.

I was a grown-ass, mature, independent woman. But I still melted when a man I was into called me *baby*.

There was no more messing around then.

I started to move, no slowness or uncertainty. I knew what I wanted, what my body needed, what felt best.

I rode him hard and fast.

Up and down, with little circles each time he was buried deep.

I didn't try to keep myself quiet. There was no need. All the businesses on the strip were closed. No one could hear as my whimpers became loud moans as I got closer and closer to oblivion.

Suddenly, the biker was pushing me back, breaking the kiss, and his hands were rough as they grabbed the hem of my shirt, and tugged it up and off of me, leaving me in my black lace bra.

It was a good one, too.

They all were.

I was a firm believer in fancy underwear. Just knowing you had something pretty and lacy and oozing sex hidden under your clothes made you walk different, I swear.

I didn't have a whole lot to work with on top, but the bra was sexy, and I'd never met a man who wasn't thrilled at the sight of tits, even if they weren't big handfuls of them.

A rumbling noise moved through the biker as he flicked the straps off of each of my shoulders, then reached behind me for the clasps, making short work of them even going in blind.

Ripping the material from me, another of those sexy little growling sounds escaped him as his gaze landed on my bare breasts, the nipples already in little peaks from the desire coursing through me.

"Don't fucking stop," he demanded, making me realize I'd stopped moving sometime around when he'd pulled off the bra. "I want to watch them bounce while you fuck me," he added.

And… *well.*

When he put it that way.

I started to fuck him again, harder and faster than before as his hands slid up my ribs, planting at the sides of my breasts, his thumbs occasionally moving out to brush across my nipples. It was a barely-there touch but it somehow made the fire inside burn hotter as I started to crest, as I got right to that edge.

Only then, as if sensing it, or feeling it, his fingers moved out, pinching my nipples between his thumbs and forefingers, that pain/pleasure mix making the orgasm slam through me, leaving me crying out and landing forward, my head in his neck as the waves crashed through me over and over.

My biker wasn't done with me, though.

I knew as I finally came back to my senses, feeling him still rock-hard inside of me.

Sensing that I was back with him, his body shifted, rolling me under him as his weight pinned me into the couch.

"I'm not done until you're screaming," he growled in my ear before he started to fuck me.

Slower than I expected at first, giving my body a chance to catch up again.

Then harder, faster, *deeper* as my legs wrapped him up, as my hands grabbed at him.

"Fuck," I whimpered, my hips rocking against his relentless thrusts. "Harder," I demanded, my hands grabbing his ass.

That growling sound moved through him, and this time we were chest-to-chest, so it vibrated into me too.

Seemingly frustrated with the limited range of motion the couch provided, he grabbed me, pulling me with him as he shifted back.

I barely had a chance to wrap my legs around him as he got to his feet and started moving.

I wasn't sure of his destination until I felt my back slam into the wall.

Then he was giving me what I wanted.

Harder.

My nails scraped down his arms as I used my leverage to try to slam down onto him as he buried deep each time, the depth borderline painful in all of the best ways.

Then the orgasm was screaming through my system, catching me so off-guard that I didn't have time to cry out, just sort of choked on the air as the pleasure moved through me in currents over and over.

"I want to hear it," he rumbled when I came back down and he was still inside of me, but moving more slowly, letting my body recover yet simultaneously somehow build back up.

His fingers were gripping my ass again, and then we were moving, turning. He was walking backward so I wasn't sure of his intentions until I felt my ass deposited onto something hard and cold.

Josie's desk.

His hands went to my shoulders, pushing me flat against it, so I could look up at him, and him down at me, as he grabbed my knees, and pushed them wide.

I was vaguely aware of her pen holder tipping over, and pens and pencils dropping and scattering around the floor.

I was too lost in the moment to care.

He spread me wide on the desk, his gaze moving over me, the heat and hunger in his eyes making my pussy clench around his cock again.

There was nothing, I was sure, as hot as a man you were into looking at you like you were the only fucking thing in the world.

His one hand stayed at my knee while the other one slipped up my inner thigh, then moved between, his thumb teasing gently across my clit.

"Fucking perfect pussy," he murmured. Then, when my hips did an almost involuntary wiggle against him, wanting more friction, a smirk tugged at the corners of his lips. "Fucking greedy too," he said. "Guess I gotta give it what it wants."

There was no more talking then.

Just fucking.

Hard and deep and fast.

But this time with his finger working my clit.

With his other hand toying with my breasts, then slipping upward to circle around my throat. Just a possessive pressure at first, holding onto me like he owned me.

And in that moment, *he did.*

But as my pussy tightened, as my moans got louder and more uninhibited, his fingers dug in, cutting off just the right amount of blood flow as the orgasm slammed through me.

The result was the screaming orgasm he'd been seeking.

"There it is," he growled, fucking me through it. "That's a good fucking girl," he added, and those words alone seemed to drag out the orgasm until, finally, he slammed in hard, his body jerking as he came too.

I wasn't sure how long we stayed there like that. My entire fucking body felt like it was buzzing. And I couldn't seem to muster any muscle strength if I wanted to.

I was just dead weight on that desk, trying to bring my breathing and pulse back to something resembling normal.

It helped that the biker seemed equally as affected, his own chest rising and falling quickly, his eyes closed, his head tilted, trying to bring all the pieces back together, so he could function once again.

Everything came back into focus slowly, then all at once.

Like how fucking stupid I'd been to take him in my office. I could have fucked him in an alley. At a motel. On the fucking beach.

Anything but in the one place that actually led back to me.

The plan formed even as I was trying to push up on the desk.

He was in my way, though. So I pressed my boot-clad feet into his stomach, and pushed him back, feeling a small bit of regret as he slid out of me, knowing that this had to be the last time.

"What's the—" he started.

"Come on. We have to get out of here before the owners see something on the cameras and call the cops or something," I lied, climbing off the desk, yanking my skirt down, then rushing in the back toward the couch, where I bent down to retrieve my shirt and bra.

The shirt I put on.

The bra, I balled up in my hand.

"What..." he started, brows pinched, confused.

Which was the plan.

"Hurry *up*," I hissed, fisting my panties too, then making my way to the door. "Put your cock away," I demanded, getting to the door, then making a big show of looking out both ways, like the owners or cops could be right around the corner.

"The fuck is going on?" he asked, but he was coming closer even as I heard his zipper slide into place.

"Breaking and entering isn't going to look good on my record," I told him, moving outside, then waiting for him to do the same, before closing the door. "Okay. This was fun. Catch you around!"

Then I turned and all but sprinted away, weaving up and down different streets until I was sure there was no way he could follow me.

"You good?" a voice asked, making me turn to see the bouncer outside of a kinda rinky-dink bar. No line. No flashing lights shows. And the only music came from a jukebox that people had to pay to play. Whoever had the most quarters seemed to be playing metal that screamed out of the gaps under the door.

"Ah… yeah," I said, nodding. "Don't mind me," I added, flipping my bra over my shoulder, unraveling my panties, then slipping them on under my skirt.

"No, sweetheart, I don't mind at all," he said with a smirk that said he both liked my boldness, and knew what I'd just done. At least vaguely. "You need help with that?" he asked as I pulled the bra off my shoulder.

It was not quite as easy to get a bra back on under your clothes as it was your panties, but I managed well enough. Without flashing the bouncer. *Much.*

"Am I going to catch anything drinking out of the glasses in there?" I asked, looking dubiously at the door. "'Cause I could use a drink."

Or five.

Maybe ten.

Whatever it took to try to permanently wipe that biker's perfect smutty amazingness out of my mind.

It turned out it was twelve drinks.

Until I all but blacked out in the back of a cab before dragging my ass back to my apartment.

Still, though, as soon as the light cut through the windows in the morning like little hot knives stabbing into my hungover eyes, the visions of the night before came flooding back.

There was no forgetting that biker.

Even if I didn't even know his damn name.

Chapter Seven

Cato

Dazed was the best way to describe how I felt as I drove my ass back to the clubhouse after the fuck in the building we'd apparently been trespassing in.

I couldn't quite tell you if it was because the fucking had been so good—which it was—or if it had more to do with the abrupt brush-off afterward.

Again.

It was enough to give a man a fucking complex.

Even if I knew she'd had a good time.

There was no faking those kinds of orgasms, the way her pussy squeezed my cock over and over, how she stiffened, how her breath caught before the cries escaped her.

She'd had a great fucking time too.

But still, somehow, she wanted to get rid of me as soon as possible after.

I still didn't know her fucking name.

I wouldn't go so far to say I felt used. That was ridiculous. We were both consenting adults. We both chose to engage in casual, no names, sex.

That said, I felt… disposable.

Or maybe that wasn't even fair.

The fact of the matter was that I wanted more. And she was denying me it. Which made me feel like a fucking petulant child being told they couldn't have another cookie when they really wanted one.

I didn't have a right to demand more from her.

And I couldn't get all bent out of shape when I'd happily taken what had been offered.

I sighed as I climbed off my bike, reminding myself that it was useless as fuck to harp on it. Seeing the woman twice was incredibly lucky and against the odds. Seeing her a third time was almost impossible.

It was over.

I had to fucking move on and accept that.

It helped that by the time the guys rolled in the next morning, the OG guys were already around, talking about the new prospects, and a game plan for getting together during the open house to discuss first impressions.

"You're home?" Huck asked when I'd rolled down the stairs.

"Yeah. Wasn't feeling the club," I admitted, shrugging. "You need anything special from me today?"

"Just keep your ears peeled. Figure the other guys are going to be hungover as fuck, so it's good that you'll be sharp," Huck said.

"And, let's face it," Seeley said. "Levee is going to look for partying buddies. There's nothing wrong with that, but we want brothers who are capable of doing the job and who have good heads on their shoulders, not just someone who can throw back shots."

"Got it," I agreed, nodding. Seeley had probably always been the driven and focused member of our group. Levee was the most laid-back and fun. I was more of the moderate one. At least when it came to work shit. No matter how down for fun Levee was, I could never get him to jump off a bridge with me.

"How many guys are we expecting?" I asked.

"Twelve or fifteen," Huck said.

"But we're hoping to get a solid two or three new prospects out of the group," McCoy clarified.

"Got it," I agreed, nodding.

"But if everyone agrees the pool is good enough, we're not opposed to four or five," Huck added.

"Okay," I agreed, glad to have something else to focus on other than my mystery woman.

The guys came rolling in then, bleary-eyed and sleepless. But within an hour, they were showered and caffeinated, and Eddie was at the stove, getting food going.

"Sounds like the party is starting," Levee said as we heard the rumble of bikes and the slamming of doors.

Being an avid biker wasn't exactly a prerequisite. I'd never been one before joining the club. Neither had the OG guys. But, inevitably, we all learned to love the freedom of bikes. The solace you found in taking a long ride when you needed to clear your head. So we weren't going to hold it against the guys who were showing up in cars.

Another couple of hours later, the awkwardness and formality was long gone. The club girls were around, happy to have new meat to flirt with.

Food was scattered around the counters.

Liquor was flowing.

"Cato," Huck called, jerking his head at me.

Walking over toward where he was standing with

Seeley and McCoy, I nodded. "What's up?"

"Gonna need you to get a feel for Coast and York," he told me, discreetly motioning in each of their directions.

York, for lack of a better way to describe him, looked like a fucking lumberjack.

Tall, wide, fit, with a brown beard and hair.

He had a serious air about him, but he had a girl on his lap.

Mature enough to be a valuable member of the team, but also down for a good time.

Coast, on the other hand, had 'crazy' tattooed all over him. Tall, but a lean kind of fit. Borderline skinny, but with abs. His hair skirted that line between brown and blond. His eyes were a piercing blue. The man had children's blocks tattooed on his collarbone that spelled out 'Fuck You.'

So... less mature.

More scrappy, judging by the fresh cuts on his knuckles.

The "Fuck You" blocks weren't his only tattoos, either. There were ones on his chest, arms, and back—which I could see because he was in the pool, chasing around a couple of squealing women—and even on his neck and side of his face.

"Are those roman numerals what I think they are?" I asked, meaning the ones on the side of his face. Thirteen, it seemed.

"Yeah, so it seems," Huck said, shrugging.

Meaning he'd taken thirteen lives.

It wasn't an astronomical number. For a lifelong criminal, anyway. But it was up there.

"They're going to put on their best show for us," McCoy reasoned. "But if you can integrate yourself a little more…"

"Right," I agreed, nodding. "On it."

And with that, I decided to actually try to join in on the party, having a few drinks to loosen myself up, then making my way over toward where Eddie was talking to York.

"Hey, man, there you are," Eddie said, smiling. I swear I'd never seen the man in a bad mood. "Was wondering where you were. This here is York. York, one of the brothers, Cato." We exchanged the typical chin-nod thing that practically had the gregarious Eddie rolling his eyes. Never having struggled in social situations, Eddie could never understand when people didn't just strike up immediate connections. "York was just telling me about life in rural New York state," Eddie said.

"Yeah?" I asked. "What's it like up there?"

"Cold," York said, shrugging.

"Roll with any interesting crews?" I asked. "We have connections up in Jersey, so we know a thing or two about the world up that way."

That was mostly a lie. Sure, Huck knew about some of the shit up that way, having spent time there himself, but the rest of us were in the dark.

"No, worked for myself," he said, shrugging it off.

"Chopping down trees?" Eddie asked, all charm and affability. "Look at them arms, man. You could be like that dude online that chops up big hunks of wood while dirty-talking 'em. Drives the honeys wild," he said, before walking away. Likely to go check on something he was cooking. Despite there already being enough food to feed an army around.

"He's not wearing a cut," York said.

"No," I agreed. "Eddie is more of a… hangabout. He's trying to get full citizenship. He doesn't want to be associated in any official way to the club because of it."

"Makes sense," York said, nodding. "Let me guess. You're here to see if I'm a good fit."

"We're all here to see if you'd be a good fit," I reasoned.

He said nothing to that.

"Between me and him, isn't it?" he asked, jerking his chin toward Coast.

"Got a problem with him?" I asked, though I was impressed he was that intuitive about the whole situation.

"Depends on the crew. Too many of him, you have a problem. But one or two of him, you have controlled chaos."

"How old are you?" I asked.

"Thirty-five," he said, shrugging.

He came off as wiser than that.

"You're York, right?" Alaric asked, coming in at the man's other side.

"Yep."

"This is Alaric," I said, getting a nod from York.

"And I'm supposed to take you to the range," he said.

To that, York finished his beer, then followed Alaric without another word.

"Got anything?" Seeley asked, coming in at my

side.

"He talks like someone who's been around and has seen some shit," I said.

"Yeah. From what I gather, he's been involved in the world since he was fucking toddling."

"How so?" I asked, wondering what kind of organized crime could be going on in rural New York state.

"His old man hid bodies for the mob," Seeley said.

"No shit?" I asked, brows raised.

"No shit," he said, nodding. "York came recommended by Tony Barelli," he added.

Tony Barelli was the local mafia boss that Donovan had worked with once upon a time. A friendly, but dangerous man who seemed to take a liking on the club since Donovan had mended bridges with him a while back.

"Why? Tony made it clear he gets rid of bodies the old-fashioned, Florida way," I said. Meaning by feeding them to the gators.

"Dunno. Some sort of connection through the mob in that area. Seems like the New York crew has someone in the family to take care of bodies now, which seems to have put York out of business."

"And now he wants to be a biker? Different business."

"Steady business," Seeley said, shrugging.

"Was he already living down here? Or did he just come to try to prospect?"

"No. He was down here. His gramps was sick. He came down to take care of him. Ended up staying since he had no work left up in New York."

"Well, I… tentatively like him. He's the opposite of Coast, it seems like. Even he knew that. But he seemed to think that Coast is good people if you have more rational people around to balance him out."

"Alright. I'll let Huck know. It's gonna be harder to get a read on him," Seeley said, nodding toward Coast, who had a woman thrown over his shoulder, and was chasing another one through the shallow end of the pool.

He wasn't wrong.

In my experience, guys like that, the in-your-face, wild sorts, they seemed like they carried everything on their sleeve because they were so extroverted. But, in reality, there was a lot of shit buried deep. And that was the important shit.

"Levee'll figure something out," I reasoned.

Sure, Levee was generally pretty light and fun, but he hadn't survived his youth working for local gangs without picking up on how to read people and situations.

"Why these two and not the others?" I asked Seeley.

"It's not that it's not the others. It's just who Huck thought made the most sense. He's open to other opinions."

"Who is the guy with the gauges?" I asked, nodding over toward a man at the side of the pool, sitting on the end of a chaise, seeming to have some deep conversation with one of the club chicks.

He was tall and fit with black hair, a matching beard, dark eyes, black ink, black clothes, gauged ears, and a black hoop nose ring.

Seeley looked for a minute, brows pinching. "I don't remember him being invited," he admitted. "Go strike up a conversation. I'm gonna check back with the others."

I grabbed three fresh beers, and headed over.

"Ceerie," I said to the club girl as I approached. "Refill?" I asked, holding out a beer to her.

The interruption seemed to shake whatever serious mood had been hanging around her. "Hey, Cato," she said, giving me a warm smile. "I'm going to go say hi to Eddie," she said, seemingly desperate to get away now that whatever spell this guy had on her was broken. "Nice talking to you," she added, though she sounded mixed on that.

"What was that about?" I asked, taking Ceerie's seat, handing the guy another of the beers I was carrying.

"She was telling me about how her mother used to beat her as a kid," the guy told me, making my head whip over.

The fuck?

"That's not exactly party talk," I said, confused. Ceerie was a party girl through-and-through, always light and fun, never having any sort of serious conversations with anyone, not even if the party was dying down, and people were having drunken heart-to-hearts; she always tried to lighten things up again.

"I kind of have that effect on people," the guy claimed, shrugging. "A skill, if you will. Often, not one I like having, but..." he said, waving outward.

"What's your name?" I asked.

"Velle," he said, holding out his hand.

"Cato," I supplied.

To that, he nodded, then looked off at the party as a whole. "So, Cato, what's her name?" he asked, and I couldn't stop myself from glancing in his direction, finding him already smirking at me, like he knew he was right.

A skill.

Yeah, that seemed a good way to put it.

An asset, even. For the club. Maybe not so much for his personal life.

"Whose name?" I asked, feigning ignorance.

"Doesn't take a genius to see you haven't spared a woman here a second glance all night. There's a lot of them," he added. "And they're all pretty. So what's her—*his?*—name?

"I'm not seeing anyone," I insisted.

"But you want to be?" he asked.

"Alright, Doc," I said, exhaling hard. "Enough about me. You're the one who should be doing the talking here. Why do you want to join the club?"

"My old man was in a club. Not a one-percent club," he clarified. "Spend most of my life in a clubhouse. Especially after my ma ran out on us. Sometime in my teens, though, he stopped going. Which meant I stopped going. I dunno. I always kind of missed it. But I'm not looking for a hobby, a place to drink and bitch with friends. If I do it, I want to make a job out of it."

That wasn't a bad answer. And it was always good to have someone around who knew how clubs worked. Even if the outlaw aspect was unfamiliar to them.

"What do you do now? Or what have you been doing?" I asked.

"Well, up until three months ago, keeping my nose clean to stay off my parole officer's radar," he admitted.

"What'd you go away for?"

We didn't have a lot of hard and fast rules in the club, but crimes against women, children, or anything to do with drugs were big no-nos for us.

The last one less because of morals, and more because addictions got... complicated. And we needed things decidedly not complicated with our men, considering how delicate our line of work is.

To that, Velle snorted. "I went out with the wrong woman. Who happened to 'belong' to some rich and powerful fuck in the area who accused me of stealing his car. I thought it was her car. I was taking a drive with it while I waited for her to get done at the nail place. Got slapped with a grand theft auto and did three years."

"She didn't defend you?" I asked.

To that his brows raised, like I was asking a stupid question. "Don't think she had much of a choice in the matter when she belonged to a man like that."

I was going to make sure we had Arty confirm his story, maybe even look into that guy and his girl. But I kind of liked Velle. And it wouldn't hurt to have someone in the club who had a knack for getting information out of people.

"How was it inside?" I asked.

"Eh, it was... inside," he said. "Sucks at first, then you get used to it. Got bunked with a shrink who got charged with giving out meds for a price. Learned some interesting shit from him."

"The kind of shit that has party girls admitting to being abused by their moms?"

"I didn't fucking hypnotize her or some shit like that," he said, shaking his head. "But if you just know how to… guide a conversation and ask the right questions… people will tell you anything you want to know."

To that, I nodded, figuring it was probably true. Especially if someone had a couple drinks in them. And Ceerie was always drinking at parties.

The woman who was currently piggy-backing on Coast in the pool as he tried to blast another club girl with a foam water gun each time she popped up out of the water in a different location, smile plastered over her face, seemed like a completely different one from the serious, vulnerable one who'd been sitting with Velle just moments before.

"So, the P.O. situation…"

"Over," he told me. "I even moved and got new numbers after it was over," he said.

"Okay," I agreed, nodding. "And you know how prospecting works?"

"Used to be forced to do chores with the prospects of my old man's club back in the day. Figure shit isn't that different here."

"And guns…" I said.

"What about 'em?"

"Do you know anything about them? Can you shoot?"

"Dad was a… let's call him a hobbyist," he said,

but the way he looked off to the side and shook his head said that maybe his dad was a little bit less of a hobbyist, and a little more obsessed with the cold, hard metal. "I was holding a rifle before I could even walk," he added. "Learned to shoot young. I'm no one's sharpshooter, but I can hit a target."

I liked his honesty.

I was no sharpshooter either.

But that was what we had Alaric for.

"Have I passed the test?" he asked when I had nothing else to say.

"You've... piqued my interest," I said. "But this isn't my decision. How'd you hear about this open house?" I asked.

"The club in town was talking about it."

"What club in town?"

"The other MC?" he said, brows pinching, confused by my confusion.

"Like your dad's MC?" I clarified.

"No..."

The fuck?

How had another club moved to the area without us knowing?

"What town?" I asked, trying to sound casual.

"A couple over. Coral Springs."

"Oh, yeah. Of course. Thanks. Alright, well, I'll put in a good word with the president," I told him, clinking my beer to him, then making my way away, trying not to seem rushed or upset by anything, knowing Velle was good at picking up on that sort of shit.

"Inside," I hissed at Seeley and Huck as I got close.

74

"What's going on?"

"First, my vote is for Velle. With the gauges," I said. "Second, he just informed me that there's another one-percent MC over in Coral Springs. When the fuck did that happen?"

I could tell by the way Huck looked to Seeley that he had no idea either.

The problem was, even Seeley looked surprised. And Seeley knew fucking... everyone.

"I'll look into it," Seeley assured Huck. "Maybe pay a visit to Arty to check things out."

To that, Huck nodded, but I had the feeling we would be hearing a lot about this moving forward.

"So why Velle?" he asked.

"Grew up in an MC. Regular kind. But he knows about how they work. Just got off of parole from grand theft auto, though he was technically innocent on that. Might want to have Arty check into that story too, though," I told Seeley who was already shooting off a text.

"The thing was, when I walked up, he had Ceerie confessing all sorts of personal shit about her childhood. But when I interrupted, she almost seemed... shocked that she'd admitted it. He said he spent time in a cell with a shrink and... picked up some tricks."

"Mind-fuck kind of tricks," Huck assumed.

"It seems like it. Just figure... that's an interesting tool to have at our disposal. If his story checks out. And you guys get the same feel," I said, shrugging.

"We'll check him out. Thanks, Cato," Huck said, clapping a hand on my shoulder.

Then, feeling like I'd done my job for the night, I went up to bed and tried uselessly not to think of my random woman. And the way her pussy clenched my cock when she was turned on, when I talked dirty to her, when she came, crying out. And how much I wanted to hear her crying out my *name*.

She was still on my damn mind several days later, when we were having another party, but this time a sort of… welcoming party for the new prospects.

York.

Coast.

Velle.

Though some of the other guys had another two names in mind that we just wanted to look into more.

I was doing my best to try to actually be at the party, enjoying myself.

Then a hand was touching me.

And, like a fucking fantasy come to life, there she was…

Chapter Eight

Rynn

"Why do you keep staring at my desk?" Josie asked several long, hot, sexually frustrating days later, making me snap back to the moment, and shake my head at her.

"I'm not," I insisted.

I mean, I wasn't a monster.

I made sure the next morning, nursing a skull-crushing migraine, that I got to the office before Josie to use a couple of bleach wipes on her desk, gather her pens and pencils, spray the couch with disinfectant, and get rid of the trash with the condom in it.

But no amount of cleaning and sanitizing could wipe the memories from my damn brain.

I couldn't remember what I had for breakfast two days ago, but every sordid little sexy detail of fucking in my office several days before was etched into my memory.

"You okay?" Josie asked, brows pinching. "You've been kind of strange for days," she added, not one to mince words. She knew I didn't need that from her.

"Yeah. Just a little..." I said, waving a hand at my head. "All over the place," I decided. "The heat is getting to me," I added. She didn't know that the heat I was talking about was the kind between a woman and her very sexy, anonymous biker.

"You've lived here your whole life," she said, rolling her eyes at me.

I hated almost everything about the heat. Always had. I was a Halloweeny, spooky chick who craved a cool breeze and fallen leaves.

Alas, I seemed incapable of leaving Florida.

I guess, in a way, in my line of work, living somewhere that was familiar to me was key. If I needed to make a getaway, I knew all the side streets, or the abandoned buildings I could enter and hide out, even which places I might find people willing to hide me out until the heat burned out, and I could go back to my life.

I'd feel really lost and vulnerable in somewhere more suited to my personality. Like New England. So I was stuck in Miami. At least until retirement. But, honestly, chances were I was a native for now and ever. But I could always aspire to living in New England for the autumn, then heading home before the frigid days of winter set in.

Maybe I could get a second home up there for visits.

But that meant hustling even harder while I could.

And that I needed to get my head off of the hot biker and onto the job.

"You sure you're alright? I don't want you taking this job if your head isn't in the right place," she added, ever my mother hen. You know, in the best way. Which was… nice. I hadn't exactly gotten that from my own mom, so having a friend around who gave a shit about me meant a lot.

She was right, though.

That was the problem.

This wasn't a job where I could be off my game.

This wasn't an hour in a club.

This was something that required planning and close contact with people who would not like what I was doing if they found out.

And by 'not like,' I mean that I would end up sliced in several thick chunks of flesh and fed to some hungry alligators.

No evidence.

No way to get justice.

And, even worse, possibly putting sweet Josie at risk.

It wasn't an option to go into this job half-cocked.

I had to plan, which I'd been doing for about a day and a half.

But then once the planning was done, I needed to execute it. And I had to be sharp. On my toes. Ready for anything.

I was starting to worry that wasn't going to be possible for me.

Unless…

No.

God.

That was a ridiculous idea.

"I promise I won't do the job until I am sure I am in the right place," I told Josie.

"Okay," she agreed, nodding.

"You going to head out?" I asked as she started to rearrange her desk.

"Yeah. I have a hot date with the bookstore," she said.

"Text me when you get home," I demanded as she got up to check that Binx had enough food and water to hold him over until the morning. "Maybe I'll drop by after to get you," she said, rubbing under Binx's chin for the two-point-five seconds he allowed that before he started to swipe at her.

"He'll be fine," I reassured her.

He had more than enough space. And he generally loathed all human contact, so it wasn't like he would be lonely.

"Yeah, I know. I just feel bad for him."

"He spends his time at your apartment tucked under the couch, avoiding you," I reminded her.

"That's true," she said, nodding. "Alright. Are you heading out too?" she asked as she grabbed her purse.

"Yeah. I'll walk you to your car."

It was still reasonably light out. But I was paranoid about Josie's safety. She was just so darn… soft. Innocent. I wanted to protect that at all costs.

From there, I hopped into my own car, doing some more scoping things out, shoring up my plans.

And losing my focus about every ten minutes.

It was freaking infuriating, to be honest.

I'd never struggled to focus on a job before.

Especially not a job as important as this one.

There was no way I could go through with the next phase the way my mind was right then.

"Damnit," I hissed, slamming my head back on the rest as my fingers squeezed the steering wheel over and over, trying to talk myself out of it.

In the end, though, my hand went to the ignition button and my foot slid to the accelerator.

And I was driving.

I didn't even have to look it up. Because my stupid, horny ass self had already looked up the address of the clubhouse online. Just in case.

Really, I couldn't think of a single other way to get my head back into the game but to fuck the guy again.

It wasn't an especially long drive to Golden Glades, but the roads got increasingly desolate as I went, making it feel like it should have been further from Miami than it was.

Sometime as I was closing in on the clubhouse, my phone dinged, telling me that Josie was safely home, and asking if I was okay.

I paused outside the open front gates of the clubhouse—which was, surprisingly, an actual house —to text her back, telling her all was good, and to enjoy her new books.

Then I pulled fully in, seeing the line of motorcycles as well as a smaller row of cars. A couple of them some fancy-looking sports cars.

Even with the windows up, I could hear the music thumping from somewhere in the backyard. Other noises came from that direction as well. Squeals and laughs. Loud splashes.

Party noises.

I guess I'd picked a good night to drop in.

No one would be suspicious of a random chick hanging around a party. They wouldn't try to look into me, and figure out who I was.

Grabbing my purse, I climbed out of my car, my gaze scoping out all the exits. Something I'd been unconsciously doing since I was a kid.

You always have to know how to get away, Rynny.

That was my uncle talking.

I took everything he had to say to heart.

I didn't go toward the front door, not when the party was out back.

"Oh, hey, bud," I said as I was met by a giant-ass tortoise who was munching happily on some flowers. "Are you supposed to be here?" I asked. He had no answers. I figured I would find someone reasonably sober and mention the big dude, just in case he wasn't supposed to be outside.

The party was in full swing in the backyard.

Bikini-clad girls were in the pool. One or two of them were actually topless, entertaining some men who were happy to give them their attention.

There weren't a lot of men around, actually.

I counted all of seven, maybe.

One of them was standing at the grill, flipping skewers full of meat and veg.

The grumble of my belly said I wouldn't mind swiping one of those. But I wasn't there to eat. I was there to... be fed, if you will. My body had been starving since the last time I'd seen him.

"Hey, honey," the man at the grill greeted me, giving me a warm smile. "You looking for someone?" he asked.

"Actually, I am looking for..." I said, walking toward him, and grabbing his arm. "Him."

Thankfully, he was right there. Because it would be a little uncomfortable to admit I was looking for someone whose name I didn't even know.

"Damn..." the man at the grill said, shaking his

head sadly as my biker turned at the unexpected touch.

"The fuck..." he said, eyes going wide.

"Yes," I agreed, smirk toying with my lips. "Let's fuck," I said, grabbing his wrist, and pulling him with me toward the back door of the house.

He followed behind as I walked into a nice, oversized kitchen with a seating area to the side. And, unexpectedly, a parrot cage.

"Fuck... you... Benny," a macaw ground out between bites of pasta someone had left on the table.

Speaking of pasta, there was a serving bowl of it on the counter. Along with quesadillas, chicken with cheese and salsa, and various other finger foods.

These guys sure knew how to party.

No pizza and freaking pigs in a blanket for this crew.

"Hell, yeah, fuck that Benny," I said in a sing-song voice to the bird who just kept chowing down on his stolen pasta. "There's a tortoise on the side of the house," I remembered to say.

"He lives here," my biker said.

"Okay. Good. Now that that's out of the way, take me to your room," I demanded, pulling him toward the stairs.

He let me, following a step behind, then at the top landing, grabbing me, and slamming me back against a door, his lips and hands already on me.

His cock was straining almost immediately, pressing against my stomach, intensifying the ache I felt to have him inside of me again.

When his hand slipped under my skirt, I

shamelessly let him finger me right there in the hall. Where anyone could see.

I didn't care.

I just needed more of him.

More of this.

Every nerve ending felt fine-tuned to his touch as his fingers slipped in and out of me, thrusting, twisting, his thumb finding my clit and moving side to side.

"Fuck," I whimpered, rocking against his touch. "More," I demanded, not sure what I was asking for, just knowing this wasn't enough.

He dropped down in front of me then, pulling my leg over his shoulder, yanking my panties to the side, and feasting on me, his tongue circling over the hood of my clit, but not making direct contact as his fingers moved in and out of me again.

"Fuck," I cried, my fingers crushing into his skull as he worked me. "Just like that," I cried, head tilting back on the wall, eyes closing, getting lost in the moment. "Don't stop," I pleaded.

But I didn't need to.

He had no intention of stopping.

Not until I was crying out, my legs going weak, thighs shaking, as the orgasm slammed through me.

He worked me through, it dragging it out until my legs felt like they weren't going to hold me anymore.

He came back up, hooking an arm around my waist, and hauling him against me as he walked me to the side, pushed open a door, then kicked it closed as he led me in.

I was too much in an orgasm daze to pay attention

to anything but the way he was backing me into the
room until my legs hit the mattress.

I lay back as he came over me, his body crushing
mine in a way I couldn't have anticipated wanting so
badly, as his lips claimed mine.

Hungry, but unhurried.

Taking his time.

I should have been impatient, clawing at clothes,
demanding he fuck me into oblivion, so I could get
back to my life and focus again.

But I just… melted into it as his lips pressed and
his tongue caressed. I went with him as he rolled me
over him, so his hands could roam up and down my
back, sinking into my ass, but not with the same
urgency as before.

Still, my desire was building again. Slower,
somehow deeper, more intense.

Every inch of my skin felt overly sensitive, like
when you got a sunburn and ran your finger over it.
God, yeah, that was it. It almost *burned* I was so turned
on.

His hands snuck up under the hem of my shirt,
teasing over my bare skin, making goosebumps
prickle, and a shiver course through me.

Impatient, his hands went back down, grabbing my
legs, and positioning them to straddle him as he
folded up.

His hands went down again, grabbing my shirt,
and pulling it off of me, the material flying with a flick
of his wrist to the side of the room.

That rumbling noise I loved so much moved
through him as his hands glided up my sides, then

skimmed under the lacy beige and black bra I had on.

He worked the clasps free, then pulled the bra off, tossing it in the direction of my shirt, and baring me to him.

The cool air in his room had my nipples tightening into points, drawing his attention.

The next thing I knew, his hands were there. Squeezing. His thumbs and forefingers were next. Teasing.

My hips did a little involuntary wiggle against him, his hard cock pressing into me, promising fulfillment. But, for a change, I wasn't in a rush to get there. I was enjoying the hell out of the journey.

But that didn't mean my hips didn't continue to writhe as the biker's hands moved over my breasts, then leaned down to suck one of my nipples into his mouth, creating a white-hot spark of need that spread from the contact and outward until it completely overtook me.

Suddenly, my own hands were greedy, pulling at his shirt until he moved back, and allowed me to remove it and the cut that was over it.

I expected him to be damn near perfect.

I'd felt enough of him to know he was built. And he was. Gloriously so. All those thick muscles of his arms and chest, and the little caverns between the ones in his abdomen.

Damn near but not actually perfect

Because there was a nasty scar on his stomach, puckered and pink.

A gunshot wound.

My fingers caressed down his stomach, watching

the muscles twitch, then circling my fingertip over the scar tissue.

My hands moved back up, pushing into his shoulders until he went flat. Then I was teasing him, running my lips down his chest, stomach, over the scar.

My fingers made quick work of his button and zip, then reached inside to draw out his straining cock.

There was hardly a pause before I had him in my mouth, feeling a little thrill of desire as his breath hissed out of him as his hips bucked up into my mouth, and his hand slammed down on the back of my neck.

Not much was quite as hot as a powerful man losing control because what you were doing to him.

I got high off of his pleasure as I worked him.

It wasn't long, though, before he was gathering my hair in his hands, and using it to pull me back over him.

My lips sealed to his, kissing him hard and long as his hands stayed lost in my hair.

But then he was moving, rolling me back under him again, and moving away to sit on his knees near my feet.

Reaching out, he grabbed my skirt and panties, dragging them down my legs, leaving me completely bare below him.

Finished, his gaze moved over me, taking his time, relishing each exposed inch. I wasn't sure I'd ever felt quite so exposed and vulnerable with a man before.

Then he was leaning down again, running his lips up the inside of my ankle, my calf, knee, thigh, belly, chest, neck, then finally to my lips as he shifted his weight to remove his pants and boxer briefs before his body pressed back down against me again.

His hard lines met my softer ones, his cock sliding against my pussy, teasing, as he reached out, grabbing a condom from the nightstand, then moving off of me just long enough to slip it on.

This time, when his weight pressed into me, his cock slid deliciously inside of me, settling deep as we both let out a gasp of pleasure.

I don't know how long we just looked at each other, just lost in the moment, in each other.

But my body was aching for more as I wrapped him up in arms and legs, pulling him more tightly against me.

"Move..." I begged, wiggling against him.

"Cato," he murmured.

Damnit.

I didn't want a name.

That made this personal.

But, then again, what about this *wasn't* personal?

"Say it," he demanded, voice rough.

"Move, Cato," I said, watching the heat slice across his pretty green eyes.

But then he was moving, and that was all there was in the world. Our bodies connected, the pleasure building.

I built slowly, almost painfully too.

But when the orgasm moved through me, it was at an unhurried pace as well. Deep, slow pulsations of pleasure that had me crying out and arching into it, into him.

His lips were on mine after, soft and coaxing, like his still-hard cock inside of me.

It wasn't until I was whimpering and writhing again that he started to move more, fucking me harder and faster, driving me up once again.

But before I could come, he was grabbing me and flipping me onto my belly. His hands dug into my hips, yanking them up and back toward him while my front stayed on the bed.

He surged back inside of me, the position intensifying the sensation as he fucked me harder still, his hand slapping my ass, then the other going down to wrap my hair around his hand, doing little tugs, the little pains making the pleasure multiply until I was on the precipice again.

His hand slapped, my hair got tugged, and his cock surged deep.

And I fucking... shattered.

And I was pretty sure I cried out *his name.*

"That's a good fucking girl," he ground out as he fucked me hard for another moment before slamming deep, and coming with a groan.

I came back slowly, collapsing onto my side, looking off at the room, trying to ground myself, get my head on right.

It was a surprisingly roomy space with deep green walls that, as someone who liked all things dark, I approved of.

The bedding was all black, and I had to give the guy props. He not only had extra pillows, but an actual *headboard.*

God, what was it with guys not having headboards

and only one pillow?

The bar was on the floor, I swear.

But this guy—Cato, I reminded myself—was raising it with his great color scheme, good quality bed, dressers, and nightstands, and the fact that the place was reasonably clean.

I needed to stop finding reasons to appreciate a man I was just using for sex.

It couldn't be anything more than that.

I wanted to say that I *didn't want it to be more than that*. But I wasn't sure that was exactly true anymore.

The fact remained, though, that I couldn't have more.

So I just had to get over that desire.

"Be right back," Cato said, giving my ass a little slap, then climbing off the bed, finding his pants, dragging them mostly up, then walking out of the room.

Presumably to the bathroom.

I didn't hesitate.

I rolled off the bed, yanking up my skirt, and throwing on my shirt, then fisting my bra and panties, shoving my feet in my shoes, and rushing the fuck out of the room, trying to creep over the floorboards as I heard water running in a bathroom.

Then fucking *booking it* down the stairs, through the front of the house, out into the driveway, and into my car.

I don't think I sucked in a proper breath until I had the engine on, and was peeling out of the driveway and onto the street.

I didn't look back.

I couldn't.

Because some part of me knew that if I did, if I saw him there, that I was going to throw all my rules out of the window.

As ridiculous as that was.

Chapter Nine

Cato

She fucking… ran out when I was in the bathroom.

And she would have had to run, too. I was too fast for a slow walk out of the clubhouse. She'd fucking booked it to the driveway.

By the time I got to the window to look out, she was already pulling down the street.

"Fuck," I sighed, dropping down into bed after, smelling that chocolate and coffee scent of her all over my sheets. It was going to make sleep impossible. But I couldn't bring myself to strip the bed and wash her smell out of my bedding either.

I'd barely ever spoken to the woman, but I was somehow more into her than anyone else I'd ever come into contact with before.

What the fuck was that about?

Maybe it was just the mystery. The unknown. That wasn't something I was used to either. Maybe if I just knew her damn *name* I wouldn't be so up in my head about it.

She was still what was on my mind the next day when Huck caught me coming downstairs where he and McCoy were already cleaning up the clubhouse.

"Hey, got any plans today?" he asked.

"No. Got something for me to do?" I asked.

"Want to head over to Arty's and ask him about the

Velle guy? And the new club?" he added.

"Sure."

I mean, it wasn't my idea of a great time. I liked Arty, don't get me wrong, but his place was a sty. I would end up hauling out black bag after black bag full of trash teeming with fuck-knew-what to the dumpster while he clicked away at his keyboard, all but ignoring my presence.

But, it was something to do other than let my daily thoughts about my mystery woman eat me alive.

"Seeley will probably meet you there later," Huck added.

"Alright. Anything specific you want me to ask?"

"Nah, you know Arty. He deep dives into it. He'll tell us more than we could ever think to ask."

"Okay. I'll head out after I get some coffee," I told them.

Then I did.

And the fucked up thing? The whole drive, all I could focus on was that I'd be back in Miami. Where I could possibly run into the woman again. Even though I knew that was fucking ridiculous.

My knock on Arty's door went unanswered. Which wasn't uncommon. He got lost in his work. Everything else ceased to exist.

When I reached for the knob, though, it turned in my hand.

"Christ, Arty, you've got to at least lock your fucking door," I lectured as I moved inside, the door sliding a row of cans out of the way as it opened. "You work for all sorts of fucking unsavory people," I added, walking right over to a window to open it up, heat be damned, because the place smelled rank.

It was as expected.

The bed was unmade, the sheets needing washing desperately. The garbage can—one of the outdoor variety, an attempt one of the women likely implemented in the hopes that the trash wouldn't end up all over the floor and tops of surfaces, an effort that failed it seemed—had several flies dancing around on top.

I went over, closing the bag, then tossing it out of the door, so I could go back in and start collecting the shit on the ground, dressers, and around the computer desk where Arty was steadily working, completely ignoring me. I knew from experience that it was pointless to interrupt him until he took a break.

So I continued to clean, dumping iffy contents of old coffee cups into the toilet, then cleaning the bathroom, stripping the bed, sweeping the floors, everything to get the place even halfway decent again.

"Hey, man, don't get too distracted, okay? I'm just gonna take this shit out, drop off your laundry to be cleaned, grab some coffee, and come back."

He said nothing, and I had no idea if he even heard me, but I headed out regardless, wanting to get this shit handled.

The girls who were with the OG members all took a liking to Arty, dropping in to clean when they could, making sure he ate something decent. But the girls were busy with kids and shit like that, so they hadn't been dropping by as often as they used to.

It was lucky the prospecting period included a shitton of cleaning. It gave me skills that my upbringing hadn't provided me. And it made me a lot less squeamish about rolling up my sleeves and doing the dirty work. Though, no, none of the work I'd done at the club had been anything as disgusting as Arty's place.

After dropping off his laundry, I headed out to grab some more cleaning supplies, garbage bags, ordered lunch, and got some coffee.

By the time I came back, Arty's headset was off, and he was looking around his apartment like he'd never seen it before.

"You got floors in here, man," I said, handing him a coffee and a bag of food. "I think I'm as amazed as you are," I added, setting the sheets on the bed, but not putting them on.

"You never come here," Arty said, brows pinched.

"I think I only got to come because I was up first," I admitted. "We have a couple of things we want you to look into," I told him as he handed me a sandwich, then bit into his own.

"Like what?"

"First, a new MC over in Coral Springs. We don't even have a name, but someone mentioned it, and it was the first we'd heard of it. But also, I want you to look into an ex-con named Velle. Sorry, that's all I got. Woulda gone away for grand theft auto. Got off of parole a few months ago."

"It's enough. Velle isn't a common name. I'll find him."

"Great," I said, nodding.

"He's prospecting?"

"Probably. Actually, can you look into his old

prison bunkie too?" I asked. "He was a shrink that went away for giving scripts he shouldn't have. I'm just curious if there was anything else shady about him too."

"Okay," he agreed, tearing into his sandwich like he hadn't eaten in days. Given how gaunt he was, that was probably true. When he was working, Arty tended to drink, not eat, his calories. And he was always working. Most of the food containers that were in his garbage were mostly full. Hence the smell. And the flies.

"Been busy, huh?" I asked.

"There's a lot of work lately," he agreed.

"Have you had any days off?" I wondered, feeling a stab of guilt at piling more work on. But the fact of the matter was, Arty was going to be working no matter what. I don't think the man had any hobbies or friends, or even left his apartment much. Knowing him, he even had all his coffee and energy drinks ordered in and dropped off outside his door.

Maybe we should make more of an effort to try to get him to hang out at the clubhouse, come to some parties. Maybe meet a girl. But I also knew that it wasn't his scene, and forcing him into it was only going to upset him.

If nothing else, I guess I could try to hire someone to visit every week to clean. Or twice a week, given how bad it was. It would put my mind at ease to know his place wasn't at risk of a roach or rat infestation. The man made more money than likely all of us combined. He shouldn't be living in his own filth.

"How've you been, man? Haven't seen you in a while."

"Got a new system," he said, waving toward his desk.

"Yeah? How's it going?" I didn't give a shit about computers, but this was what he was into. The least I could do was engage him a bit to talk about it.

"Good. Teddy brought me to the store," he added.

"When was that?"

"A month ago."

He'd probably had the place cleaned then, too. There was no way Teddy would walk into his sty of a home, and just let him return to it looking like that. And aside from the garbage, the place itself—the walls and baseboards and such—were all clean.

"How's Teddy been? I haven't seen him." Everyone else had, when they'd been hitting the clubs and crashing at one of Teddy's penthouses or mansions. But I'd been keeping to myself. And pining over a chick whose name I didn't even fucking know.

"He's Teddy," he said with a shrug.

Teddy was closer with the OG guys than the rest of us, but he came from money, and only managed to acquire more of it throughout his life. The only reason he'd ever gotten to know the club was back before it was a club, and he'd been passed out in the back of a car that Huck and the guys had jacked.

"Does he come around often?" I asked.

"Every couple weeks or so. I don't know. He takes me places."

Because Arty didn't drive. I didn't know if he had a license or not, just knew that he didn't have a car. And when he hardly left his apartment, I guess it made sense not to, even if he could drive.

There was a ding on Arty's computer.

And just like that, I lost him.

The rest of the sandwich went uneaten, but I left it with him when I said I was going to pop out for a bit, then come back to see if he had anything for me.

When I did, I'd get rid of the sandwich.

No more festering fucking foods.

I texted Teddy while I was walking down the street, asking if he knew of any cleaning companies that would handle working on Arty's place while he was in it.

I'd like to claim that it was unintentional, that I was just… taking a walk and wound up there.

But that would be complete and utter bullshit.

I intentionally walked in that direction, retracing the steps I'd taken the night after the club.

Because something had been niggling at me the more I thought about it.

That she didn't have enough time to pick a lock before I saw her. Not even if she was really fucking good at it.

But she would have had time to slip a key into a lock and turn it.

I tried to keep my pace casual as I passed, eyes forward, knowing that the window or the office that mirrored back to me my likeness was probably one-sided. And I didn't want her to spook before I could at least make it inside.

I pushed the door open, and was met almost instantly with a brighter version of the room I'd fucked the woman in. The dark walls, the black decor, and the slightly out of place brightly colored details on the top of the sole desk in the place.

Behind that desk wasn't my mystery woman, and I tried like hell not to feel deflated by that.

This woman was objectively just as pretty, but in an entirely different way. Short, slight, with a chest that was pushing against the confines of her brightly colored sundress. Her hair was strawberry blonde and just as vibrant.

She was the antithesis to everything else in the office.

"Can I help you?" she asked, tone bright, but I didn't miss the way she'd stiffened, the nervous way she was eyeing me up.

And, yeah, I got that.

I was a big guy.

She seemed to be alone in the office.

There was the threat of danger there.

"Yeah, actually," I said, nodding, but not approaching, not wanting to make her anymore uncomfortable. "I'm looking for someone I thought worked here," I said. "She's—"

"Either Binx has learned how to open packaging, or *someone* is going to need to answer for my cheddar popcorn being all gone," a voice said, moving closer. A familiar voice. Even if I'd hardly heard it say anything at all to me that didn't involve asking me to fuck her harder, or begging me not to stop. "I am in a… what the *fuck*?" she griped as she walked into the office, holding a—presumably empty—black bag of cheddar popcorn.

The woman at the desk's gaze moved between the two of us several times as her hand slipped, sliding open a drawer.

"It's okay, Josie" my mystery woman said to the other one. "You don't have to tase him. Yet," she added, eyes boring into me. "What the fuck are you doing here?"

"I was about to ask the same thing. Since the last time we were here, you claimed we were breaking and entering."

"I…" she started, searching for a lie to feed me.

"I had a feeling, though, that no matter how good you might be, you couldn't pick a lock that quickly. So I came to see if my hunch was right."

"Wow. Stalker much?" she asked, raising her brows at me.

"I think you're the one who tracked me down to my clubhouse just so you could get a quick fuck again, then ran out before I could get back from the bathroom."

"What? Are you butt-hurt that I left? Get real," she said, but I got the feeling she was putting on an act. "I mean, men can use and discard women left and right, but the second a woman tries to play that game, someone's in their feels about it and is showing up at a woman's work like a complete creep."

"I, ah, should I leave?" Josie asked, looking between the two of us.

"No," the woman said at the same time that I said, "Yes."

"I'm getting sorta mixed signals here, Rynn," she said, and I got to watch as my mystery woman's eyes slid closed as she took a deep breath.

The mystery was over.

I had a name.

Rynn.

Unusual. Which was fitting.

Rynn sighed.

"You can go take lunch," she told Josie.

"Are you sure? I could just grab something quick, and bring it back..." she suggested, shooting a quick look in my direction.

"Don't worry," she assured her friend. "We both know that I'm the dangerous one here," she added, crumpling up her empty bag, and shoving it into the trash beside Josie's desk.

"I'll bring you back more popcorn," Josie assured her as she grabbed her purse. "Are you sure..."

"Yes," Rynn cut her off. "Go on. I'm fine."

We both stood there in silence as we watched Josie get up and leave.

Then we both turned back to face each other in unison.

"So it's Rynn, is it?" I asked, feeling like I'd just solved my life's biggest fucking mystery. But having no idea what it meant for me moving forward.

Chapter Ten

Rynn

So it turned out that fucking Cato *did* work to clear my mind and allow me to focus.

I'd gotten more work done after leaving the clubhouse and when I got up after a few short hours of sleep than I'd been able to do in days.

The problem was, it seemed like sex with him was a short-acting drug. And by the time it wore off, I was left feeling foggy and frustrated and in need of every kind of junk food I could find.

I'd torn through half of the dozen donuts that Josie had brought into work with her that morning, then the animal crackers I had stashed in the cabinet, a coffee and grilled cheese I'd ordered in, and had still been jonesing for the stupid white cheddar popcorn.

Like mass amounts of carbs and fat could somehow clear my head. And take the place of toe-curling, voice-box-aching sex.

Don't get me wrong, I've always enjoyed sex. I mean, if you didn't like orgasms… something was wrong with you. Their entire purpose was to feel good.

That said, I'd never been so fucking ravenous for an O before. Not to the point of being unable to focus on anything else.

I mean, sure, if you were getting some good dick,

you could find your mind wandering here and there throughout the day, and even start to get a little hot and bothered by those thoughts.

This was different.

It was obsessive.

I felt like I was going to crawl out of my skin unless I got him inside of me again.

Maybe that was the difference between good dick and world-class dick.

Because Cato?

That man was fucking exceptional in bed.

He could do hard and fast and ruthless. Could spout dirty things that didn't give me secondhand cringe. But he could also be slow and soft and intuitive.

Still, though.

Once in a twenty-four-hour period should have been enough to sustain me.

Somehow, though, like a drug, it seemed like the more I got, the more I wanted.

It was absolutely ridiculous, but I felt like I could overdose on him and it still wouldn't be enough. I could be holed up in a hospital bed from sex-related exhaustion or some shit like that, and still be asking the nurse if she could sneak Cato in for a quickie.

It was getting out of control.

I *felt* out of control of my own mind, body, and desires.

I'd even been telling myself that morning as I tore through all the junk food readily available, that the only way to break a habit like this was cold turkey.

Sure, there would be a period where I was moody

and aching for him. But, eventually, the urge would pass, and I could function again.

Then the bastard had to go and start using his head, thinking about things, then acting on those thoughts. Bringing him into my office. Where Josie got to hear him talk about using and discarding him.

I knew her. And all her romantic musings. She was probably getting ready to come back and talk to me about how she thought it was so romantic that he came for me, that he was hurt about me running off after sex.

She was probably already planning my wedding.

Macabre, gothic romance elements.

Black gown, of course.

Oh, my God.

Now *I* was thinking about my wedding.

I didn't want a wedding.

My plan was to die with a bunch of sugar babies who would mourn the sudden loss of my money, if not my wrinkly self. And cats. There would be cats involved. I would leave everything I owned to them.

I definitely didn't want a spouse.

I couldn't think of anything I'd want less, in fact.

I shook off those thoughts, looking back at the man himself. Surprised by the surge of relief that moved through me.

And, damn, did the man look good in the daylight. I got to see all that stupid good-looking-ness.

"So, it's Rynn, is it?"

Ugh.

My name had no right to sound that good coming out of his mouth.

"Names don't matter," I said, lying.

"No?" he asked, head cocked to the side. "Mattered to me when you were moaning my name last night."

"But you had no need to know my name," I said. "Things were working fine without that."

"Were they?" he asked, brows pinched.

"For me, yes," I said, shrugging. Only partially lying. Not exchanging name and numbers complicated things. It meant that, at first, we had to rely on fate to bring us together. Then, my own desperation to drive out to Golden Glades for a little sex session. Life would be easier if I could just text him to come over for a little stress relief.

"What's the matter, Rynn?" he asked, taking slow steps toward me. A predator stalking his prey. "Worried you'll get attached if we know names and numbers?"

"Oh, please," I scoffed, crossing my arms over my chest, pretending a little shiver didn't move through me as he got closer.

"Sure ran off like you were scared of something last night," he said, stopping right in front of me, standing close enough to force me to crane my head up to keep eye contact.

"What the hell could I possibly be scared of?" I shot back.

"Catching feelings."

I let out a mocking laugh at that, rolling my eyes for good measure. "Get over yourself, Cato," I said.

"Rather have you over me," he said with a sexy smirk before he was bending down, snagging me behind the knees, and yanking up. A little squeal escaped me as my arms grabbed for him instinctively as he lifted me off my feet, holding me against him, then walking me backward toward the couch.

There was none of the exploration of the night before.

Hands roamed, gripped, slapped.

My lips pressed, his tongue teased, and his teeth nipped.

I was pushed damn near to the edge before his hands even slid up under my skirt, toying with my clit in an unhurried pace, before two fingers slid inside of me. My hips rocked against his touch, needing more, needing the feel of him.

Pulling away, I kicked out of my shoes, reached under my skirt, and pulled down my panties, watching as Cato pulled out his cock, stroking it a few times, then sliding on a condom as he watched me.

I was about to climb over him again when I suddenly thought better of it.

Because as much as I scoffed at the very idea, some part of me was actually worried about catching feelings.

It wasn't something I'd ever needed to worry about before, but there was a real potential of it now.

Enough that I was worried about forming an attachment through sex, something I was usually able to disconnect emotions from.

So instead of moving over him, I turned, then moved to straddle him, but facing away, suddenly needing that disconnect.

Cato said nothing, likely just excited that I was the experimental sort, and started to rub his cock up my pussy, teasing across my clit until I was whimpering and writhing again, finally getting lost in the moment and out of my own head.

His cock shifted back, then slid inside, and the position had him stroking across my G-spot as he settled, making a deep moan escape me.

I paused for just a moment before I started to ride him, working him quickly, keeping myself in the moment and out of my head, getting lost in the sensations as his fingers dug into my hips, guiding me to go faster and faster as the orgasm started to build.

It crashed through me with an intensity that had me crying out and falling back against his chest, gasping for breath.

As usual, though, Cato wasn't done. He was still hard inside of me.

"You gonna give me another?" he asked, his deep voice in my ear, his warm breath tickling the shell of it, making a little shiver move through me. Not an inward one, either. One he felt. One that had a little approving rumble moving through him.

Then he was shifting, taking me with him as he gained his feet.

His hands were on my hips, holding me close, keeping his cock inside of me, even as my whole upper body bent forward, my hands landing on the coffee table to steady myself as he started to fuck me.

Hard.

Fast.

The sounds of us filling the room, quickly drowned out by my moans, and Cato's groans as we built up together.

"Fucking perfect pussy," he hissed, making my walls tighten in response. "You gonna squeeze my cock again?" he asked, even as my orgasm started to crest, and then do just that.

Taking him with me this time.

"Fuck, Rynn," he hissed afterward, his hands still on my hips, and I was pretty sure that was the only thing holding me back from falling forward right then, because my hands weren't even on the table anymore, just hanging limply in the air as my body hinged away from Cato's.

Seeming to realize this, his hands went around my belly and chest instead, pulling me backward against him, then just holding me there.

What's more, though, was I let myself be held.

When was the last time I'd been held like that? Hugged, even?

Months?

I mean, if drunken girlish friendship hugs didn't count... never?

I was pretty sure I'd never just been held by a man before.

To be fair, there was a good chance that was because of me, not them. Maybe I'd known several men who would want to hold me close, but I was always the one creating a disconnect, never wanting to get messy feelings that would fuck up a good, casual situation.

This, though?

This felt good.

That gooey chocolate in the center of a warmed lava cake kind of good.

I tried to remind myself that it was all the sex hormones creating a feel-good cocktail in my body.

The thing was, I'd had sex before. And I don't ever remember anything like this.

Which was precisely why I needed to pull away, damnit. But I couldn't seem to force my limbs to do so.

In the end, it was fate that forced us apart.

And by "fate," I mean Binx.

Who, apparently, had jumped silently on the arm of the couch only to reach out his evil paw, and take a swipe at Cato's ass.

"What the *fuck*?" Cato groused, yanking away from me to spin around and find the cat sitting there on the arm, daring him with his yellow eyes to come closer.

There's more where that's coming from, human.

Binx was a fan of scratching the shit out of you.

You sat too close to him? Bloodshed.

You fed him three minutes too late? Better go find some antiseptic.

You were in his general vicinity when he wanted nothing to do with you? You better hope the medical kit still had butterfly sutures.

He was the epitome of a cat who barely tolerated humans so he could get free, easy food.

Poor Josie was always scratched to shit because of him. I'd been burned enough times to know to let the dude live his life without interference from me.

"He's not a fan of people," I told Cato as he stared at the cat, confused why he ended up with a scratch on the ass when he hadn't done anything to him.

"Great office mascot," Cato said as I yanked my panties up.

"Bathroom is through there," I said, pointing. "There should be stuff to clean the cut with," I added. "You want a treat, you little asshole?" I asked Binx in a sing-song voice, heading into the kitchen to get him one.

I took my sweet-ass time in there, too, tossing little fish-shaped treats onto the ground as Binx kept giving me dirty looks, pissed that I made him walk around to pick them up.

"I'm thinking of your waistline, my dude. You don't want the vet to tell us to put you on a diet, do you?" I asked.

"You're sweet talking him when he took a chunk out of my ass?" Cato asked, leaning in the doorway, watching.

"Maybe I should trust his instincts," I said, shrugging.

"Please," Cato said, shaking his head.

"Please, what?" I asked, small-eyeing him, just knowing he was about to say something that was going to piss me off.

"That cat's opinion of me isn't going to make you stop craving my cock, Rynn."

The thing was, he wasn't wrong. And *that* pissed me off.

"Oh, get over yourself. I can get cock anywhere I want," I said, putting the treats away in the cabinet. And having another sudden urge for my popcorn. And maybe some pizza.

"Yeah?" Cato asked, closer than he should have been. And when I turned back, he was right behind me.

"Yeah," I said, craning my neck up to keep eye contact.

"Then why'd you drag that pretty ass of yours all the way over to Golden Glades to get some of mine?"

"I was in the area," I lied. I was good at it. My job relied on it.

"Liar," he said, voice small.

"Why would I lie about that?"

"Because you don't want to admit that I have any kind of power here," he said, surprising me.

I mean, couldn't he just be a pretty meathead? Did he actually have to have thoughts and feelings and powers of observation?

He was right.

I did always like to be the one in power. In everything, really. In work, that's why I worked for myself. In friendships, that's why I only had Josie, who was okay with that quirk of mine. And absolutely in relations with the opposite sex. It's why I didn't date anyone seriously.

I was always the one to initiate, to walk away when I was done. I had never had a guy in my apartment.

I liked things casual and fun.

And up until now, there'd never really been the threat of someone having any sort of power over me to control my feelings and actions.

But he was right.

I had dragged my ass all the way out to Golden Glades when I had casual fuck-buddies on my phone right in town who could have provided a quick, no-strings fuck.

I'd gone to him because I couldn't freaking think

straight with how much I wanted him.

That was dangerous.

It was threatening my very equilibrium.

"Need I remind you that you came and hunted me down at work today," I said. When you didn't have a good argument, you could always just deflect. People tended to scramble when they were the ones with accusations thrown at them, forgetting all about the ones they'd tossed at you.

"The difference here being, baby, that I don't have a problem admitting I'm intrigued."

"By what? My 'perfect pussy'?" I asked, air quoting his words from earlier.

He didn't rise to the bait.

A slow, wicked little smirk toyed at his lips, though, and I swear my knees felt a little unstable seeing it.

"That, yeah. Pretty sure I'm never going to get enough of that," he admitted. "But I didn't mean your pussy. I meant you."

Ugh.

There was more of that gooey feeling inside.

"I'm not interested in that," I told him, but my voice sounded hollow even to my own ears.

"Why not? Too chickenshit to admit you might be into me?"

"I don't even know you," I reminded him. Because that was true. I didn't. He was a guy whose dick I liked to ride. That was it. I'd only just recently learned his name for God's sake.

"But you want to," he said, too damn astute for his own good. Amazingly good-looking guys were supposed to be dumb. It was, like, a rule of the universe, damnit. He was defying the laws of nature. "And that scares the shit out of you, doesn't it?"

"I'm not scared of anything," I said. Because, for the most part, that was true. I lived on the edge. Very little freaked me out enough to make me think twice about doing it.

Except, of course, those pesky things we liked to call 'emotions.' Those I avoided like the plague.

"No?" he asked, and I didn't trust the look in his eye then. "Then meet me at Turner Loop tomorrow at seven."

"Seven what?" I asked, curious despite my better judgment.

"In the morning."

Turner Loop was an area in the Everglades.

"For what?" I asked.

"Show up and find out," he said, then leaned in closer to add, "Or be a chickenshit. Your choice, baby," he said, then turned and walked out.

Of the kitchen.

Then the office as a whole.

When I finally walked out of the kitchen, Josie was standing there behind her desk, eyes bright, smile knowing.

"Don't," I pleaded, accepting the bag of popcorn she held out to me, and taking it back to the couch, where I dropped down and started eating it by the handful.

"He's incredibly good-looking."

"For an outlaw biker," I admitted.

"Right. Because you are *so* concerned about people

being on the right side of the law," she said, rolling her pretty eyes. "It seems like you have been holding out on me," she said, coming over to bring me a soda, then stubbornly standing in front of me. Waiting for an explanation.

"I fucked him a few times," I admitted. Because, well, she was my best friend. My only friend. This was what we did. We talked about my sex life.

"Umm... no," she said, shaking her head.

"Umm... yes. I have his handprints on my ass, if you'd like to check," I said, watching as her cheeks went the tiniest bit pink. Josie was no prude. Not with those books she read. Some of the shit in there could make *me* blush. She just blushed over everything. It was sweet. "Really, I'm not shy," I added, playing into her blush and starting to roll a bit to my side.

"I can take your word on that, thanks. I'm not doubting you two—"

"Fucked," I supplied for her.

"Yeah. It definitely seems like you have. But the thing is... you kept it from me. And you don't ever keep that from me."

"I told you! The high speed chase on the bike, remember?"

"Yeah, but you didn't tell me you two hooked up again after that. And that kind of tells me there's more to it than just sex."

"Literally. It has just been sex. He only knows my name because you told him."

"I think, if it was just sex, you would have told me about it. So I think you're worried you might actually like this guy."

"I don't like that I was feeling like I couldn't focus because all I could think about was banging him," I said.

"Why would it be such a bad thing to be interested?"

"I don't do relationships. I'm focusing on work. So I can retire and acquire half a dozen sugar babies to bring me margaritas and massage my feet."

"But you're going to show up at Turner Loop tomorrow," Josie said. Not asked. Said. She was sure of it.

"I won't even be awake at seven in the morning," I reminded her.

Why then did I drag my ass to bed at ten instead of after two like I normally would?

I didn't even let myself ponder that as I drifted off to sleep.

Chapter Eleven

Cato

I'd never been in a position of trying to coax a woman into acting on her feelings for me before.

I'd never wanted to.

I couldn't even explain to myself why I was insisting on this shit. But I wanted more. And I was going to see if she genuinely did too.

Borrowing the club's SUV, I drove my ass down toward Turner's Loop at the crack of dawn the next morning, not wanting to miss her if she showed up before me.

But as an hour slid to two, I was starting to think she wasn't who I thought she was. Someone who would see this invite as a challenge, and would have too much pride to back down from it.

I was about to slide the kayak into the water to go by myself when I heard it. The crunch of footsteps.

"You're late," I said without turning, trying to seem casual.

"No," she said, making me turn to find her standing there in her usual black skirt and combat boots. She had a cut-off black tank on, and I could see the straps of her bikini peeking out. "I was here. Just debating if I was just going to leave, or come over here and accuse you of trying to make me *exercise* at seven in the morning."

"Baby, I only brought one paddle," I said, reaching for it to show her. "This was more of a 'curious to see if she will agree to kayak through alligator-infested waters at seven in the morning' thing," I admitted.

"In that case..." she said, moving past me and toward the kayak.

I pushed it into the shallow water, then waited for her to get closer.

"You're in front," I told her, then watched as she pretty effortlessly climbed in. "Done this before?" I asked, curious because she didn't strike me as the water hobby type.

"I grew up in Florida. I've done all the water things," she explained. "I've enjoyed almost none of them. So congrats on your choice of activities for the day," she said, shooting me a smirk over her shoulder as I started to paddle us into the river.

"There's a life vest on the floor in front of you if you want it." She didn't reach for it.

"Alright, fine," she grumbled after we moved along the water slowly and silently for ten minutes. "It's pretty out here," she admitted.

It was.

Sure, there *were* alligators. And there was a risk because of them. But not a super serious one. I'd chosen this more because it was fucking beautiful around these parts with the trees shading the water, and the overgrown grasses lining the banks.

It was empty this time of day too. And, you know, because we weren't actually allowed to kayak here. There were special tours for that kind of thing. This was not that. But there was no one out here to bitch at us about it anyway.

We had it all to ourselves.

I figured it would be a good test for if we clicked or not. I guess I just hadn't anticipated how bad we both were at this. How inexperienced we both seemed to be at dating.

That was what this was, too.

I couldn't even try to deny it.

This was a date.

I'd set up an activity.

I'd even packed a lunch.

Eddie had prepared it, giving me raised brows but encouraging words as he did so. "Sometimes you gotta wine and dine the right honey, man," he said, nodding. "They appreciate effort."

Aside from a few awful and awkward attempts in high school, I'd never been on an actual date before. Sure, I met women. And we may have even occasionally shared a drink or a meal, but it was never planned. I didn't set it up. And we both went into it knowing it wasn't going anywhere serious.

This, though?

I don't know.

I had a feeling that there was something here. Something more than mind-numbingly good sex. Otherwise, I wouldn't be doing this.

"Did you grow up in Miami?" I asked, knowing that one of us had to get the conversation started.

"Born and raised," she agreed, nodding. "You?"

"Yeah. Know that neighborhood I drove us to that first night?"

118

"I do. I got hit on ten times when I was walking to my ride," she admitted.

"Don't doubt that," I said. "I grew up there. Me and two of my now club brothers. Used to scout for the local gangs as kids. Which is why I can still drive through there doing a high-speed chase without issue."

"The gangs just… let you become a biker?" she asked, dubious.

"We were never officially initiated. It was just kid work we did. Bunch of the kids in the neighborhood scouted or ran errands for money but never actually joined the gangs."

"Why not, though? Isn't a MC kind of just the same thing as a gang?

"In a way, yeah. I think the MC just has more of a family vibe to it. Something we were all kind of looking for," I admitted.

"I know a thing or two about family dysfunction," she agreed. "My mom's a fucking psycho."

"And your dad?" I asked.

"Oh, big finance bro. Lots of fancy lawyers who somehow got him out of paying child support *or* having to see me growing up," she said, but somehow without a trace of bitterness.

"You're not pissed about that?" I asked.

"Oh, dude, I don't waste time on getting angry. I just go ahead and get even. When I was sixteen, I wanted a car. I'd been busting my ass working to save for one. But my aforementioned psycho mom found and drained my account just shy of when I'd have what I needed," she told me.

"What'd she use it for?" I asked, thinking maybe it was to pay bills. That didn't make it right, but it was at least a halfway decent reason.

"Oh, to fund a girls trip to the Caribbean. Which she left me home for, mind you," she said. "Which worked out in my favor, because there was no one to get suspicious when I spent a full week stalking my father."

"Stalking him for what?"

"To catch him cheating on wife number two," she said. "He had a cheating clause in his prenup. Which was really fucking stupid for someone who cheated on wife number one *with* wife number two. But it worked in my favor. A couple of photographs and a threat to tell the wife's lawyer landed me a much nicer car than the one I wanted."

"You blackmailed your own father?" I asked, feeling my lips curve up. "That's pretty fucking epic."

"I know, right?" she agreed, shooting me a smirk over her shoulder.

"What kind of car did you take him for?"

"A black Corvette convertible. Fifty-something grand seemed to cover a few years of those missing child support payments," she said. "God, I loved that car. Not because of the car per se. I don't give a shit about cars. But because of how I got it. That was a rush."

"I'm assuming it didn't work out with wife number two?" he asked.

"No. I mean, that was probably because I made an anonymous phone call a few weeks later, telling her where to catch him cheating for herself. I got my car, she got her money, and my old man got to move onto wife number three. Worked out for all of us."

I could see her doing all of that, too. Even at sixteen, I imagined she was a little badass. Probably a little more mad at the world than she was now, because weren't we all back then? But just as sure of herself and daring.

"Ever talk to your dad again?" I asked.

"Not in any sort of meaningful way. I wasn't looking for a connection. I don't see any reason to beg to be in someone's life if they clearly don't want you there."

"I get that," I agreed.

"So, what was your family life like?"

"Had a dad who drank too much. And when he did, he got angry. Usually at me. Had a hateful mom with a cigarette constantly dangling from her lips. Would constantly tell me how I'd ruined her life. And because of that, she riled up my old man's temper when he got home from work, then directed him at me."

"That sucks," Rynn said, shaking her head a little.

"Yeah. It was pretty common in my group of friends. So we all hung together to avoid going home to our fucked up families."

"So the MC is like your found family."

"Yeah, something like that," I agreed. "Don't think any of us knew what we were missing until we found it."

It was nice, though. Having people around for holidays or special events. When I was down with a gunshot wound, there was always someone there to help me move around, to change my dressings, to bring me food and drinks, so I didn't have to move more than was necessary.

Sure, there were occasional moments of tradition in my upbringing. Once in a while, my old man brought home a tree for Christmas. Then he and my mom would get into screaming matches over the lights and ornaments.

When I'd broken my leg doing an—admittedly reckless—stunt on my skateboard, my mom had come to the hospital. But she'd lectured me the whole way home about being an idiot, and making her leave work to deal with me. They never took me to follow-up appointments. And my old man cut off my cast with a saw he'd borrowed from work.

It was probably why that leg ached when the weather was wet.

"Do you still see your family?" she asked. "If they're alive, that is," she added.

"They're around somewhere. In that same old building, I hear. But I do my best to avoid them. Things didn't end well. My old man and I came to blows that ended with his jaw broken. Last I heard, he got hooked on the pain meds they gave him following that. And he and my ma fell down that path."

"You have nothing to feel guilty for," she said, thinking I needed that reassurance. "It sounds like he had the fight coming after beating up on his kid. My mom was a piece of shit in many ways, but she didn't put her hands on me. There's no excuse for what he did to you. And what your mom did for that matter."

"Do you still talk to your mom?"

"I occasionally run into her. Or she will try to reach me through different numbers—because I have her blocked—to leave me long, rambling messages about what a terrible daughter I am for cutting her out of my life. As if kids who go no-contact do it for shits and giggles. Anyway, that's enough of that. What's the club like? Seems to be lots of partying."

"It can be, yeah. I have a feeling it will be more and more now. We just added some new prospects. We had been getting to the point before where it was more married guys than single, so the parties were becoming more like small get togethers."

"Really? They're married?"

"That surprises you?"

"It doesn't really fit in with the mental image I have of outlaw bikers, I guess," she admitted. "Oh, ah, that's... that's a suspicious rock formation," she said, extending a hand, pointing into the water.

"Yeah, baby, that's not rocks. That's a gator."

"A... gator. That's... ah that's not great. Shit. He saw us," she said, voice getting tight. "He's looking at us. Cato... he's..." she said, scooting backward, making the kayak wobble ominously.

"Stop moving, or we are going to be in the water with him," I warned, surprised by her rising hysteria. I mean, she was from the area. She had to have seen a bunch of them in her life.

"Why are you going *toward* him?" she hissed, scooting backward some more, her ass all but hanging off of the back of her bench. "Turn away. I have a sneaking suspicion that I am delicious. I don't want him to find out. I told him to turn around!" she called to the gator. "Eat him, okay?" she asked as the alligator pushed off the bank and started to swim.

It must have startled her, because she scooted back with a squeal, landing on her ass right between my feet, not realizing that he was swimming away from us.

"You are, by the way," I said, unable to force my smile into a straight line when she tipped her head back to look up at me.

"I am what? A big baby about alligators?" she asked.

"Delicious," I told her, watching as she tried to keep the smile in, but it was useless. "No," I snapped when she tried to pull herself up, making the kayak rock side to side. "Stay where you are now," I demanded.

"For what? The rest of the ride?" she asked, eyes narrowing.

"We're almost at our destination now. Just another five minutes or so," I told her.

That seemed to placate her as she settled against my thigh.

Or so I thought.

Apparently, she had other things in mind as she slowly turned just enough to rub her hand over the crotch of my jeans.

Then reach up toward my fly as my cock stiffened immediately in response to her. Hell, I swear all I had to do was look at her to be half-hard.

"What are you doing?" I asked as she reached into my pants, pulling out my cock, and holding it in her hand as she smirked up at me, her eyes heated, before she was sucking me into her mouth.

"Fuck," I hissed as my cock slid in.

I immediately forgot all about the paddle in my hand as she started to suck me off. Slow at first, then a little faster, careful not to move too much and rock the kayak.

"You look so fucking good with my cock in your mouth," I growled, settling the paddle across my waist, then reaching out to grab her hair, moving it out of the way, so I could watch her work me.

"If you don't stop," I said, forcing myself to start moving the kayak again, "I'm going to come down your throat, and then you won't get to feel me inside you again," I reminded her.

She made a grumbling sound that vibrated around my cock. But then she slowly released me as I picked up the pace.

I saw the destination in the distance.

It wasn't much.

But it was a place for us to go, move around a little, sit and eat in peace without worrying about falling into the water.

It was a dock a couple feet over the water. Maybe ten feet by ten feet with a ladder leading up and somewhere to tie up your boat or kayak and a roof to protect you from the unyielding sun at this point in the trail.

It technically belonged to private property, and was rented out in the past as a camping spot, with a outdoor shower and outhouse on the land a few yards in. But the place was owned by the bank now, so there was no worries about us being caught as I pulled us up, then tied the kayak up.

"Go on," I invited as I refastened my pants.

"Ah, that's a no for me, dude," she said, eyeing it dubiously.

"Chickenshit," I said, standing up myself, making the whole kayak wobble. Rynn let out a squeal, hands shooting out to the sides, holding on as I climbed up the short ladder.

Dropping onto my ass, I leaned forward, offering her my hands.

"Come on," I invited.

She eyed me dubiously for a second, but eventually chose the dock over the kayak. Likely out of fears of the gators.

As she stood, I grabbed her under her arms, and started to pull, her body coming up slowly, her intense gaze on me, both of us very aware how vulnerable she was right then.

I lifted her until she was straddling me before grabbing the back of her neck, hauling her forward, and sealing my lips to hers.

Her hands were impatient, but I kept her close, not letting her take off my shirt, or reach between us to toy with my cock again.

There hadn't been time in her office to explore, not knowing when her office mate might return.

But out here, with no one for miles?

We had time.

And I was going to use it to take my sweet ass time with her.

My fingers drifted up from her neck to stroke through her silky hair, then gently massage her scalp, something that had her lips ripping from mine on a moan as she rested her forehead on my shoulder.

Guess I found her sweet spot.

Scalp rubs.

I took full advantage of that, massaging until she was writhing against me, until her lips were exploring my neck.

Only then did my hands drift down her back, grabbing the hem of her shirt, and drawing it up and off.

My shirt followed.

Her hands were moving up my arms as mine drifted up her ribs, then backward again, this time untying her bikini top, and drawing it slowly away, leaving her bare to me in front of the water and the nature behind her.

"Fucking beautiful," I said, watching as her eyes went a little round, like she was surprised, before her lips were on mine again.

Soft and sweet at first, but getting more needy with each passing moment.

My hands went down to her hips, pulling her up slightly so she had the height advantage, and I could lean forward and suck one of her nipples into my mouth, something that had a deep moan escaping her as her nails dug into my shoulders.

I moved across her chest, continuing the sweet torment before my lips were moving between her breasts, then down her stomach.

I worked her skirt down, and she helped me slide it off along with her panties, leaving her completely fucking *gloriously* naked.

Perfect.

God, she was so fucking perfect.

My hands went to her ass, holding, then pulling her with me as I went flat on my back.

"Sit," I demanded, voice rough, as she straddled my face. "I said sit," I grumbled, yanking her down when she hesitated.

Her sweet taste met my tastebuds as I worked her with my tongue, with my lips, feeling her writhe around me, her thick thighs like a vice grip around my head.

If this was how I went, her taste in my mouth, her whimpers in my ears, suffocated by her thighs, yeah, I'd die a happy fucking man.

Her hips writhed as I devoured her, riding my face as she got closer and closer, her moans getting louder, echoing out across the empty space.

"Cato," she whimpered, her hand closing over mine on her thigh. "Don't stop," she begged.

I wasn't going to stop.

Not until she was crying out her orgasm, her thighs shaking, her weight pressing more firmly down on me as she lost control.

She scooted backward as soon as she was in her own mind again to do so, her head resting on my chest as she breathed hard.

I rolled to my side, taking her to hers. I pulled her chin up, and sealed my lips to hers once again.

Soft, exploring, waiting for her to come back down, so I could begin to drive her back up.

My hands explored then too, moving down the slope of her spine, over her ass, her thighs, pulling one over my hip, opening her up to me, then letting my hand slide between, avoiding her clit, but teasing over her sensitive skin, then slipping inside of her.

The ragged little moan that escaped her told me that she didn't need more time to recover as my fingers started to fuck her.

"I need your cock," she murmured, making it twitch in my pants as she rolled me onto my back, straddling me. She pulled out my cock as I found the condom, then slid it on, watching her as she lifted up, got into position, then started to lower down.

Her mouth parted in a silent moan as the head slipped inside her, and there was no stopping my groan as her walls tightened around me, welcomed me in, until I was settled deep.

"Baby," I said, not recognizing my own voice it was so small, as my hands dug into her hips. "You have to move," I told her, the need so acute it was painful.

Luckily, she didn't need more encouragement than that.

But this time, it was Rynn who was taking it slow, riding me almost lazily, her head falling back, her hair streaming over her chest, half hiding her breasts as she went.

It wasn't long, though, before her need was growing too, making her ride me harder and faster, her tits bouncing, her moans filling my ears.

My hand slid in from her thigh, my finger working her clit as she kept riding, getting louder and louder as her walls tightened, as she got close.

Her pussy was a fucking vice grip as she came, squeezing my cock over and over as she cried out my name.

On a strangely primal growl, I grabbed her, holding her to me as I rolled her under my weight, overcome with a wild sort of need that didn't allow me to ease her down from one orgasm before I tried to send her surging toward another.

I fucked her hard and rough as her fingers clawed at my back, as her hips started to rise up to the thrusts, needing more, loving the borderline violence of my thrusts then.

"Fuck, Cato," she cried, back arching, legs tightening. "I'm coming," she hissed, then she was, pussy damn near taking me with her this time. But I wasn't done. Not yet.

"More," I said as she came back down, as I untangled myself from her arms and legs, going to sit back on my heels, and pulling her upward, her legs on my shoulders.

She didn't tell me she couldn't.

But fuck if her eyes weren't dazed from all the coming already.

"Yes," she said, voice so soft I hardly heard it.

I fucked her slowly then, giving her pussy a chance to recover, before I was spreading her legs outward so I could watch. I caught her looking too.

"You look so fucking good when you're taking my cock," I growled, making her walls clench around me.

She liked when I talked to her. When I praised her when I was all the way inside of her. She would never admit that to me. But I didn't need her to. I could feel it in the way she responded to me.

It wasn't long until the position was just not

cutting it, making me push her knees into her chest as I pounded into her, driving her up.

"Turn," I hissed, grabbing her to move her when she didn't respond as fast as I needed her to.

Because I was close.

But I needed her to come once more for me.

"Fuck, *yes*," she cried as I fucked her hard, as I reached down to grab a handful of her hair, pulling to keep her from moving away with each thrust.

"Fucking love being this deep," I hissed, feeling her pussy tighten in agreement.

My hand shot out, slapping her ass, making her moans get louder as I fucked her into oblivion, her release almost a scream as she came.

This time, though, she took me with her.

And I swear to fuck, all I saw was white for a long moment as the orgasm worked its way through me.

We both collapsed onto the dock after.

And, eventually, I pulled her up onto my chest, kind of surprised that she not only let me, but settled in, wrapping a leg over my waist, and letting out a contented sigh.

"I'm glad you decided to come," I said, just barely managing *not* to say *Now aren't you glad you decided to come?* I hadn't known this woman long, but I was already pretty tuned in to how she would react to certain things.

"I think I'd be just slightly gladder if that cooler was up here with us, and there was something cool to drink inside of it," she admitted.

"Alright. Give me one minute," I said, untangling from her, and moving inland to the outhouse that did, thankfully, have a small garbage where I could toss the condom. The baby wipes that were in the package were half-dried out, but they did the job before I made my way back out, then retrieved the cooler.

I was still shirtless, but my pants were in place.

Rynn?

Completely fucking bare.

Just how I wanted her.

"Water or beer?" I asked, holding a selection of each out.

"Duh," she said, taking the beer, then taking a long sip. "Okay. What did you bring?"

"Well, there's no cheddar popcorn…" I started.

"Bummer," she said, but her lips were turned up. Not enough to see those fucking dimples of hers, but hinting at them.

I handed her one of Eddie's famous sandwiches— toasted rye with fresh romaine, tomatoes, some sort of honey-dijon-mayo sauce, bacon, roast beef, and swiss.

"Where did you get this?" Rynn asked after taking a bite with a moan, her long legs stretched out in front of her to use them as a serving tray for her food.

"Eddie, a friend of the club, likes to cook. We like to let him."

"He made you sandwiches? Like… he packed you lunch? That's really fucking cute," she declared before taking another bite.

"We also have homemade potato chips," I told her, producing the bag.

"No way," she said, mouth falling open a bit. "Wait… why are some red?"

"Because Eddie thinks we need more vegetables in

our diet, I'm assuming," I said. "They're probably beet or something," I told her, watching her nose wrinkle. "No, trust me, they're gonna be good," I told her, holding one of the beet ones out for her to try.

She didn't take it, just leaned in and let me push it into her mouth.

"Okay. Fine. They're good. Out of curiosity… can Eddie be hired? For events? Private events? With one customer? But said customer has a notoriously large appetite?" she asked, and this time the smile showed her dimples.

"Eddie would cook for you anytime," I told her. "All you gotta do is drop by the clubhouse."

There.

An invitation.

Now it was just up to her to take me up on it.

Chapter Twelve

Rynn

"Soooo… how'd it go?" Josie asked, nearly making me jump out of my skin as I walked into the office, not expecting her to be there. I'd given her the day off.

But, of course, she knew I would drop in to at least feed Binx and clean the litter box. So she was lying in wait, ready to pounce.

"Christ, Josie," I said, hand to my heart.

"Come on. I've been sitting here for, like, two hours already. How was it? Was it amazing? You look flushed. It was *that* good?" she asked, practically bouncing in her seat.

I raised my hand to my cheek, feeling the over-sensitivity of it.

"It's sunburn," I admitted. Cato had told me as much as he walked me to my car at the end of the… date.

I mean… you had to call that a date, right?

An activity, some food, amazing sex.

It sure seemed like a date.

Even if I was decidedly not a dating sort of girl.

"You went in the sun for him?" she asked, eyes going almost comically round.

I mean, I wasn't fucking allergic to the sun or anything, but I did tend to stay out of it whenever possible. That was why I was generally so pale.

If my cheeks were burnt, I was a bit worried about what I would find when I stripped out of my clothes later and looked in the mirror.

I'd never had a titty sunburn, but it sounded awful.

"He took me kayaking in alligator-infested waters," I told her.

Alright, fine. We were out there for hours, and we'd only seen that one alligator who seemed completely disinterest in eating us. But still.

"You went out in the sun *and* exercised for him?" Josie asked, growing more incredulous by the moment.

"No. He did the paddling. I did the sitting and alligator-watching."

"You were gone for a long time. Were you kayaking that whole time?"

"No. We found a dock and had lunch there," I told her. "And sex," I added. Because it was true. And because Josie wouldn't be scandalized about that fact.

"That must have been gorgeous," she decided. "And kind of forbidden."

"There wasn't anyone around, but yeah. It probably added to the heat of things."

Though, objectively, we didn't need any outward factors to get a fire going between us.

I mean, my thighs were aching from the sex. I don't think my thighs had ever ached from sex before.

"Are you going to see him again?" Josie asked, cutting through all the bullshit.

"He invited me to drop into the clubhouse whenever I want to force some guy named Eddie there to cook for me."

"Right. Because this Eddie guy is why you'd want to go there," she said, rolling her pretty eyes. "Come onnn, Rynn. Give me something here," she demanded, following me as I went to the couch and dropped down, feeling drained.

The sun and the sex had proven too much.

All I wanted to do was go home and take a nap.

"You like him, don't you?" she asked, hugging a witch hat shaped pillow to her chest as she looked at my profile.

That was the question, wasn't it?

The one I'd been actively avoiding asking myself since he'd left the office the day before.

The day before, though, he'd still just been a stranger who knew all the secrets of my body. Now? Now, he was a person. With a name. And a bad family history. With interests and stories and a personality.

"I think I do," I admitted.

"Think?" she asked.

"I don't know. This is new for me," I reminded her. "Before this, all that mattered was someone was good in bed and not a complete douchebag when he opened his mouth. The bar was kind of on the floor."

"But he raised it," she said. It wasn't a question, but I found myself answering anyway.

"Yes."

"So, what would be so bad about maybe exploring that more? No one is saying you need to marry him and have a dozen of his babies," she said, shrugging. "Just… see where it goes. Enjoy it."

"To what end?" I asked.

Josie looked stumped for a moment.

"To whatever natural end it has," she landed on. "Whether that means you just enjoy each other for a few months, then go your separate ways. Or maybe you fall for each other and stay together. Whatever. You can't possibly know, so what's the point in trying to figure that out right now? Just enjoy it while you have it."

That was actually the best advice she could give me.

I wasn't, as a whole, someone who could look to the future and see a man in it. Because everything about the future I constructed for myself didn't have one in it. I mean, aside from my sugar babies. But, let's face it, that was just a pipe dream, y'know?

But I couldn't fathom waking up to someone else in my bed. Seeing their toothbrush next to mine. Their clothes in my laundry basket. Their shows on my TV.

I was really accustomed to being on my own. And, what's more, I *liked* it. So trying to imagine a different future was just going to end in a headache and me telling myself that there's no way I want that with someone.

But if all I had to do was look toward the next time we linked up? I could do that.

It would also have the added benefit of keeping my head clear. Because I had to make some damn progress on this case. There was a shitton of money on the line. I couldn't screw it up.

"I think I might take that advice," I admitted, nodding.

Enjoy it while it lasted.

That sounded entirely doable.

So that was what I did.

I worked. Then, at night, I would drive over to Golden Glades and spend some time with Cato.

We exchanged numbers that first night, so sometimes I had him come out to Miami. Not to my place. That felt way too soon. But to go out to eat. To take a drive, where we would find some private spot and fuck in the car until we were both boneless and content.

We talked, too.

About the club and his brothers a lot, since I didn't have a big circle to discuss. And the more times I went to the clubhouse, the more I saw these men, so it was nice to put stories to the faces.

There were Seeley and Levee, his old childhood friends. Seeley, in a sweet twist of fate, ended up with his childhood love. While Levee was just searching for the next woman to spend a night with.

There were the older members of the club, men married with kids and businesses.

Alaric, the former exotic dancer with sharpshooting skills and a really toxic body image problem.

There were the new guys, too.

York, a big, burly guy who seemed more suited for the backwoods swinging an ax than in balmy Florida. He was kind of quiet, didn't go out of his way to say much when I was around.

Coast, well, Coast was the definition of a bad boy. He was the kind of guy who had 'bad news' tattooed across his forehead. All sex and fun and violence muddled together to form a pretty irresistible cocktail.

The club girls, half naked most of the time, were all over him. Like a new puppy to fawn over.

And then there was Velle.

Who kind of unsettled me, but I couldn't exactly say why. Every time I saw him, he seemed to be in some deep, intimate conversation with someone who seemed stripped bare and vulnerable by whatever they were talking about.

I actually kind of avoided any one-on-one conversations with Velle.

Not that it was difficult. Most of the time when I was at the clubhouse, I was in Cato's room. And a good chunk of time, we were fucking. What can I say? We liked each other a lot that way.

But there were times when Eddie—who I told I would allow to become one of my sugar babies in the future for his culinary skills—would make a big spread, and we would go downstairs to eat, making us all need to interact.

I worried at first that it might feel awkward. I'd never been in the position to be around a guy I was banging's inner circle, to get to know them, and sit across from them and share meals.

The thing was, it was surprisingly easy. Effortless, even. Like they saw nothing off about a steady woman around. But then again, the club girls were around a lot too. And the old ladies of the older members, though I hadn't really met any of them.

Cato was completely comfortable with it, too. He would often even press a hand to my hip or the small of my back, little gestures that felt oddly—yet sweetly—possessive. Like I was his.

The crazy thing was, as the days stretched on, that was what I was starting to feel, too.

Like his.

And, in turn, like he was mine.

I would have thought I'd feel anxious or uncomfortable with that information.

Instead, all I felt was a sort of... ease. A rightness.

We didn't talk about it, of course. About titles or futures or anything like that. Neither of us seemed particularly versed in the area of relationships. But that definitely seemed like what this was starting to become. A relationship.

As big and scary and foreign as that was.

The thing was, though, as much as we had started to share, there was a lot that I knew I hadn't given him yet.

Like my address.

Like my profession.

I think, typically, that was something you discussed very early on in knowing someone, but because of the unconventional way we'd ended up starting things, that had fallen through the cracks.

And now it felt awkward to bring it up.

I couldn't tell you why. It's not like he would judge me for it. Not when he was an arms-dealing outlaw biker, for God's sake.

It just felt weird to bring it up now.

I would figure it out eventually.

Until then, I had some work to do.

The day was quickly approaching to put my plans into action, and I needed to keep my head in the game, so shit didn't go sideways...

Chapter Thirteen

Cato

She was coming around.

It had become clear to me pretty quickly that I, a lifelong single man, was somehow more comfortable with the progression of our relationship than she was. Which led me to believe that she hadn't exactly been through this before either.

Rynn struck me as someone who liked to keep shit casual. Who was then in control. Of the situation. Of her feelings. Everything.

More so than that, she also didn't have any sort of social circle. She was a loner by nature, with only Josie as a friend. And I had a feeling that was more to do with Josie slowly but surely forcing her way in until Rynn just finally accepted her as part of her life.

So it was all new to her. Maybe even a bit overwhelming. You'd never know it from her outward demeanor. She was her usual sarcastic self around all the guys, but it was clear to me that she was letting everyone else do most of the talking, while she just took things in.

Still, she was getting along with everyone. Especially Eddie and Levee. The former, because of her impressive appetite and love of his food. The latter, because she had a quick wit and was good at trading barbs with Levee.

I liked having her around, too.

More than I could have anticipated.

"I'm happy for you, man," Seeley said, coming to sit on the edge of the chaise next to me, looking off at the pool where Levee and Coast were playing pool beer pong with Ceerie and a newer club girl whose name I didn't know yet.

York and Velle were off doing chores, but no one seemed to give a shit that Coast was slacking.

"Hm?" I asked, looking over.

"You and Rynn. I'm happy for you," he said. "She suits your crazy ass," he said.

He'd been around the other night when she'd admitted to a rebellious stage in her late teens when she would jack expensive-ass cars for joy rides, fill the tanks, then return them back to the lots she'd swiped them from.

And then that she'd once done a vacation where she visited all of the tallest rollercoasters on the East Coast.

She did seem to be an adrenaline junkie like me. She just had a hard limit about anything that was near alligators, it seemed.

"I'm not too fond of stingrays, either," she'd admitted. "In solidarity with Steve," she said, doing a little cross and kissing her fingers to the heavens.

I had to admit that he was right.

I couldn't have imagined, before her, what kind of woman I could see myself settling down with. But Rynn was it. A little crazy, but just as happy to hang out and watch scary movies and eat food in bed.

"Yeah," I agreed, not bothering to try to deny it. This was Seeley. One of my oldest friends. There was no reason to feel weird talking about this shit with him.

"Gotta admit I'm a little worried, though," he said, nodding a bit.

"About what?"

"That you've let her into your world, but she doesn't seem to have let you into hers."

That was true. I still hadn't seen her apartment. I actually didn't even know, technically, what she did for a living. Sure, her business said she was some kind of consultant, but that could mean literally anything. Or could just be a bullshit cover to keep the tax people off her ass for entirely different kind of work.

I mean, no consultant needed to hijack a bike to go on a high speed chase.

I think I'd just been enjoying the ease between us, and some part of me was worried that if I pressed too much, she might freak out and pull away again.

We'd get there.

I just had to be patient.

Not my best trait, to be sure, but one I could work at for her. Because the last fucking thing I wanted to do was scare her off just when I was getting accustomed to having her around.

"We'll get there," I told Seeley. "Things are new. And she likes coming here for now."

"Alright," he agreed, nodding. "I'll back off if that's what you want."

"I know you're trying to look out for me, but yeah, that's what I want. But I know who to come to if I start having concerns too."

"Always," he agreed, about to change the topic when, suddenly, four men in cuts were standing in our side yard. "The fuck?" he hissed, standing, and reaching for his gun, prompting me to do the same.

And that action had the guys in the pool stiffening.

Coast whispered something to Ceerie, then all but tossed her out of the pool, where she got up and ran into the clubhouse, dripping fucking wet.

Not ten seconds later, York and Velle came out. Then, behind them, Alaric and Remy.

Everyone packing.

The bikers in the side yard seemed unbothered by the heat, though. And one look said there were bulges in their hip area that suggested they hadn't come unprepared either.

"Get Huck," Seeley called to Velle, who rushed off to do just that.

I took that opportunity to size up the guys.

Three of them were tall and fit. The fourth was also tall, but stockier. All sported ink and dark hair. I couldn't make out their eyes from so far away, but the three of them all had similar bone structure. Brothers, maybe?

They sized us up in turn, but no one said anything, like we all accepted that this was not for us, but for our president. Who came striding back with Velle just a few moments later. The perks of building his own house to the side of the actual clubhouse.

"The fuck is this?" he commanded, and I could see Che coming from behind the bikers, his house flanking the other side of the clubhouse property.

"Heard you've been looking into me," the one in the front, a little older, judging by the slightest streak of gray in his dark hair, said, taking one step away from the other three.

Levee and Coast quietly got themselves out of the pool, Coast pulling the other club girl out, whispering something to her as he did so, and she rushed inside as well as he went to where his towel was on a chaise, and reaching under it for his gun.

"Don't know. Since I don't know who the fuck you are," Huck said, good at sounding calm and unbothered, even in a potentially dangerous situation.

"Creed," the man who must have been the president, said, as equally as unconcerned about the altercation as Huck was. "And I don't like people in my business."

"And I don't like men showing up at my place looking to start shit," Huck shot back.

How the fuck did they know we were looking into them? As far as I knew, we only had Arty on this. And Arty didn't do shit in person. It was all online research. There was no way they could have figured that out.

I hadn't checked back with Arty since cleaning his place and telling him about the jobs we had for him.

But none of it was rush work.

And Arty was a busy guy. We tried to give him a couple of weeks if we were springing something non-emergent on him.

No one had thought to pester him since our interest was pure curiosity, not concern. And he'd already confirmed the details Velle had given me about his past. Though we were still waiting on more about the shrink he'd bunked with as well.

That was the way with Arty sometimes. He had to prioritize the emergency sorts of cases. Which, as people who've brought those to him before, we had to understand.

"I'm not looking to start shit. I'm here to introduce myself, and some of my men, and let you know that if you want to know something about me or mine, you ask us. You don't go asking around on the streets."

"Fine," Huck said, shrugging. "Then tell me about you and yours."

"We're not competition to you, if that's what you're asking. Way I hear it, we are in different trades. With that comes different allies and different enemies. So if you don't fuck with us, we won't fuck with you," Creed said.

"Why this area?" Huck asked, not completely satisfied, but everyone had relaxed a little. His guys hadn't so much as put hands over their weapons in response to all of us having our own out.

"Imagine same reason you're out this way. Low taxes, cops that can be coaxed to look the other way, and a lot of areas to lose bodies, if need be. Did my due diligence. Didn't move into your turf. Didn't move into no one's turf. Fucking nothing around in Coral Springs. But us now, I guess."

"What is your business?" Huck asked. "Since you already know mine," he added before Creed could object.

"Protection," Creed said. "In many different forms."

That was… vague.

That could mean extortion. Forcing local businesses to pay them a monthly fee to keep anyone from fucking with said businesses. The shit the mob was known for doing.

It could be private security for events.

Or it could mean half a dozen other things.

None of which concerned us, though.

Huck seemed to be coming to the same conclusion, because he was nodding.

"Alright," Huck said, holding out a hand toward Creed. "I have no plans of fucking with you," he said. "If anything, I wouldn't mind if we were friendly."

Creed took Huck's hand with a nod.

"Wouldn't mind that either," he agreed. "Maybe a meet-up one day," he added, taking a step back.

"We would be interested in that," Huck agreed.

"We are still… ironing out some kinks," Creed said. "But when we get our shit handled, we'll talk about it."

With that, he turned and walked back to his men, then they all went to leave, giving us a view of their club logo as they went.

Ruthless Knights.

"That was unexpected," Huck said, exhaling hard, and rubbing the back of his neck. "Someone call McCoy and Donovan and tell them to take their feet off the accelerator. Everything is fine."

As Remy moved to do that, Seeley stepped away from me and toward Huck.

"This was on me," Seeley said. "I was asking around since we hadn't heard anything from Arty."

"I expected you to," Huck said, shrugging. "People don't usually just show up in your backyard because you put feelers out about a new organization in town."

"He's direct," Velle said, shrugging. "That's a good quality to have in both allies and enemies. You're never sitting around having to guess what they're going to do."

"That's true," Huck agreed.

"Are we really going to have a meet-up with them?" Che asked.

"Think we might try partying with them one night," Huck said. "See what their men have to say after a couple of drinks. Just because I respect Creed's bluntness doesn't mean I completely trust him."

We had a small circle in Golden Glades.

It was us and Booker's private security firm. That was pretty much it. We'd made some headway with the local mafia thanks to Donovan and now York, but I wasn't sure we could actually call them allies.

From what Huck said of our mother chapter in Navesink Bank, they had a lot of allies. Some sort of paramilitary camp, a family of loan sharks, the local cartel, all sorts of people they could go to in times of crises for help or just advice.

Even our sister chapter in Shady Valley had the local Irish mafia as allies. And even a... tentative alliance with the Bratva.

We didn't have that down here.

But it would be nice if things shook out, and we could count Creed and his crew as allies for our club.

We could use that.

Especially until our club grew bigger, since we were still small compared to the crew in Navesink Bank. And at this rate, the guys in Shady Valley were going to surpass us.

Even if or when we had big numbers of members, though, allies were always a good thing. They had different contacts, ears to the ground in other areas than we did. If they heard of a threat to us, they would tell us. And, in turn, us them.

"Hey, why we got some pretty, dripping wet honeys in here, shivering to death?" Eddie asked, moving out of the back door, likely having just come in from work. One glance at everyone gathered around with guns in their hands had him stiffening. "Everything alright?" he asked.

"You can tell the girls to come back out," Huck said. "We just met the president of another local club," he explained. "They popped in for an unexpected visit," he added, getting a nod from Eddie.

"Was it a pleasant visit?" he asked.

"It turned out better than we expected," Huck said. "Eventually, we might have a get-together with them," he added. "But things seem alright now."

"Alright, boss man," Eddie said, nodding. "Come on out and warm back up," he called to the girls as he opened the door.

They rushed back out, still wet, and shivering, but Eddie had clearly paused to get them towels before coming out.

Guns went back into their hiding places, and as Donovan and McCoy showed up, the OG guys headed over to Huck's place to talk.

"Hey, Cato," Eddie called.

"Yeah?" I asked.

"Your girl coming over tonight?" he asked, and I felt a surprising warm feeling in my chest at those words. *Your girl.* They were getting truer with each passing day. She was mine. She just hadn't fully come to that conclusion yet. "I'm asking because I'm about to head to the store, and if she's coming, I know I have to double up my recipes."

"Ah, actually, I haven't talked to her yet today," I admitted. Neither of us were really 'text all day long' sorts of people. "But she usually pops by," I added. Because that had been true since the kayak trip. We'd seen each other every day or night since then.

On the nights when she didn't want me in her neck of the woods, though, she just showed up without texting or calling.

So I was assuming this was one of those nights.

"Yeah, she's half in love with me, you know," Eddie said, nodding. "Think you better learn to cook, or you're gonna lose her to me. And I ain't even gonna be sorry about it," he added with a smile before making his way back out to his car.

The small get-together the had been going on all day became a raging party by the time night fell. Club girls, both new and old, were everywhere.

A few even managed to charm the somewhat standoffish York, one managing to sit on his lap while they talked.

Velle had another girl all to himself, the two lost in deep conversation, as expected with him. But when the girl started crying, she was smiling at the same time, then threw her arms around Velle, holding on for a while, before grabbing his hand, and leading him inside.

Coast had taken off to the shooting range with three girls. But judging by the lack of gunshots ringing out, it seemed more likely they were all fucking back there, enjoying the fact that the way the range was set up allowed them both privacy and a sound shield.

And I was sitting there, listening to the music, wondering why the fuck Rynn hadn't shown up yet.

It wasn't that she always showed up at the same time or anything, but she usually followed her stomach to the club at her dinner hour. Which was somewhere around eight or nine.

It was ten thirty.

I reached for my phone, checking the screen, just barely resisting the urge to text her to see what she was up to, if she was coming.

I didn't want to come off as too demanding or overpowering. I knew she was kind of dipping her toe into this whole relationship thing. I didn't want her to think I was suddenly trying to pick her up and toss her in before she was ready.

On a sigh, I tucked my phone away again, and went inside the house, knowing I was only going to bring the mood of the party down.

But when ten thirty became twelve, then two, and Rynn still hadn't shown up, I had to admit that I was starting to worry.

Not about her per se, but about us. About what that crazy-ass head of hers was saying to her, getting her second-guessing things.

And she was so fucking stubborn that she would listen and push me away.

I wasn't even sure how I would charm my way back in, past those walls and that uncertainty.

"Christ," I hissed, rubbing the heels of my hands against my eyes.

I was getting ahead of myself.

She was someone used to being independent. She probably didn't even think I was waiting on her. Maybe she had plans with Josie. Or had a sick cat. Or just crashed early at home.

There was no reason to assume the worst.

Until another day passed with no contact.

Until two texts and three calls went unanswered.

Then?

Yeah, then I started to worry.

Chapter Fourteen

Rynn

It was time.

All the planning and plotting I'd been doing for well over a week was going to get put into action.

"What?" I asked, brows pinching as I looked at Josie while I double-checked the knife and eye-gouger in my shoes, then clipped on this clever bracelet I'd found that detached and worked like a garrote if necessary.

"Nothing," she said, shaking her head, her gaze skittering away.

"Come on. Spit it out," I said.

To that, she let out a deep sigh. "I don't want to mess with your headspace," she admitted. When I gave her a waving motion, she relented. "I'm nervous about this case," she admitted.

Her words landed like a blow to the solar plexus.

I mean, this was Josie. She was always a little worried for me on action nights. Hell, she even worried when I was just out on research trips. It was her nature as a sort of mother hen figure.

The thing was... *I* was nervous.

That was why her words packed such a punch.

Because, as a whole, I was never bothered by anxiety about the job. Were there times when situations got tense and my body was flooded with adrenaline? Sure. But it was never really in a bad way. If anything, the adrenaline helped me focus and act and think more quickly. It never gave me pause.

Tonight, though, I was having, you know, pauses.

That was why I strapped on the chain bracelet, despite never having worn it before on a job. And I'd bought it over a year ago. It was why my car also had several items stashed under the seats or in the compartments that could be used as weapons.

It was why I was considering actually bringing a small backpack or purse or something like that with other items in it.

I liked to pack light on a job.

Certain people saw bags of any sort as a security risk. And everything about me on a job had to suggest I was anything but that.

"I've planned more for this than almost any other job I've ever done. Including that casino job. And we all know how the security at casinos is," I reminded her, trying to put her mind at ease even as her worries only managed to intensify my own.

"These are... different kinds of people," she reminded me, hunching a bit over her desk. Josie had impeccable posture. It was alarming to see her looking almost beat down over this.

"I know that," I agreed, trying to keep my voice calm, maybe even a little upbeat. "Do you want to go over my plans again?" I asked, waving toward the file on her desk.

I didn't keep files. Not after a job was done. Not on paper anyway. I had a external drive that did have tidbits of information on all of my jobs. Mostly in the case of a repeat client, not wanting to have to ask them all the same shit over again. But I did have little maps and keywords written down. For my own memory, if the job was complicated, but also to show Josie.

True, she'd never been on a job. But she was surprisingly good at finding little pockets of potential trouble, or coming up with routes I wouldn't have thought of.

We'd been over this particular plan at least a dozen times over the past two days as I was getting ready to put it into action.

"No," she said, sighing a little. "We've thought of everything," she said.

I thought so too.

Which was why my unease about the whole thing was freaking me out so much.

I should have gone out to Golden Glades at lunchtime for a little quickie. Maybe I just needed that physical outlet to shake the weird feeling.

Until Josie said something, I'd thought that my anxiety was stemming from how much money was on the line with this one. Money like that put a lot of pressure on a person. Especially when that person worked solo, and would only have themselves to blame if things went sideways.

But as soon as she spoke up, I knew it wasn't the money. It was the job. Something about it just wasn't sitting right with me.

That being said, this was the night.

It had to be.

There were no second chances with this.

It had to go right.

Which was why when I caught my reflection in the window that was mirrored on the outside all the time, but also mirrored inside at night, I didn't recognize myself.

My tattoos that I'd lovingly curated over the years were gone, covered up with some amazing tattoo concealer that didn't even come off when I rubbed it with water and a rag. The instructions told me that I would need to use some sort of oil to get it off. Which meant that so long as no one doused me in that during the job, no one would know what was hidden.

My long black hair was tucked up under a cap, and I had a pretty fucking convincing blonde wig on instead.

I might have worried about the wig if I were around women who really knew about that kind of thing. But men were clueless about them. It worked in my favor.

They tended to be pretty dense about makeup, too. Which was how my face had transformed from someone I knew, someone I was familiar with every day in the mirror, into someone else entirely.

The careful contouring, lashes, and colored contacts made me look softer, sweeter, less threatening.

I hated the stupid contacts. No matter how well I lubricated my eyes, they always felt a little scratchy. I normally wouldn't have bothered, given how much effort I'd put into everything else appearance-wise. But the weird feeling I couldn't shake had me sticking them in and convincing myself the brown color would add to the whole makeover I was going for.

Even the clothes I was wearing were different.

Gone was my usual attire—short skirts, tees or tanks, and my combat boots. In their place was a club dress that clung to every square inch of me, and boot-style heels that were open in the toe with little cutouts up the sides, so they didn't look completely out of place, but gave me room to sew little pockets in for the gouger and knife. Smaller ones than I would normally pack. But they would do the job in a pinch.

The whole look gave me either a club girl on spring break or a high-price call-girl look.

Either would work for my cover.

I pressed my hand to my stomach, trying to convince myself that the wobbling there was from not eating enough, not from nerves.

I hadn't been able to stomach much since I woke up, forcing down a cheese stick and a couple of pretzel sticks just to keep my stomach from grumbling on the job. I told myself that I would eat after. Maybe even gorge myself on whatever takeout place was open when I was done.

What I was really craving was literally anything that Eddie's creative mind and skilled hands could cook up. But that wasn't an option. Not tonight.

But tomorrow.

Tomorrow, when this was all done, and I could breathe a sigh of relief, I was going to go back to the clubhouse and eat everything he made, then fuck Cato's brains out, and be happy this was all done.

"Exactly," I told Josie. "We've thought of everything. I think there's just a lot on the line with this one, and it's making it feel different than the other jobs."

That was likely a lie.

But it seemed to placate Josie.

"Maybe," she agreed. Though Josie really didn't care about the money. She was on salary. A nice salary, mind you. With a twice-yearly bonus—one around the holidays, and another in the spring in case she wanted to take a vacation and go somewhere. She never did, of course. I imagined that money went to new bookshelves and books to fill them. But, hey, whatever made her happy. I guess they were a vacation of sorts, too.

She did know how important the money was to me, though, so I could see her thinking that was why I was off, and therefore why she felt off.

"Okay. Burner me," I demanded, holding a hand out toward her.

I never took my real phone with me on jobs. It was too risky. Too much could be gleaned from texts. Or traced back to me via the maps apps and stuff. Josie kept an entire drawer of burners just because of this. These were basic. Just a phone with no information on it that I could use in case of an extreme emergency.

Josie held out a discreet little flip phone—yes, they still make them!—and I checked to make sure all the sounds were off before shoving it into my bra. Luckily, I had a little space in the cups, unlike Josie. It would stay nestled there, irritating and awkward, until I was safely in my car and had driven around for a while to make sure I didn't have a tail.

Then and only then, I would take it out.

The ritual was the same after.

Take off as much of the disguise as I could in the car, then get back to the office to finish the job. There, I would also call Josie, let her know it was done. And, finally, call the client to let them know it was over, then go home and relax.

It's just a couple hours, I reminded myself as I yanked down the skirt that kept riding up thanks to the clingy material of the dress, took a deep breath, and nodded at Josie.

"I'm out," I told her. "Go home. I will call you as soon as I am done."

"Okay," she agreed, leaving Binx this time, likely because she was too anxious to think of him. Not that it mattered; he would be fine. Then, stopping mid-stride, she rushed back toward me, throwing her arms around me, and squeezing tight.

We weren't typically hugging type friends. Sure, if we were buzzed enough, maybe we would hang all over each other. Mostly for support, though.

"I love you," she told me.

I wasn't used to those words. My mom, the crazy woman she was, never said them. I avoided relationships of all sorts, so I never said them then.

But there was no denying them when they came out of my mouth then.

"Love you too."

"Be safe," she demanded, then released me, and rushed out.

Be safe.

That was the plan.

I waited for Josie to pull away before I closed up

the office, nodding to Binx. "See you in a bit, dude," I said, then got into my car, and drove.

Nerves rattled my bones as I drove out of my little area of Miami and toward the location of the job.

I'd been here before.

So I couldn't tell you why it suddenly bothered me that the streetlights were mostly out, casting the area almost entirely in shadow.

I knew the shadows. I'd hidden in them. Familiarized myself with them.

Now, though, they felt ominous.

As did the fact that all there was on the street was an empty, unused parking garage across the way from a building—a long, low warehouse—that I would need to enter.

It wasn't abandoned.

Maybe that was the most off-putting part.

Most of the times I'd scoped out the area, there had been no cars, no noise, nothing. Because I didn't want to be spotted, so I avoided business hours.

Now, though, you could hear music, the chatter of raised voices to be heard above it.

The warehouse wasn't a warehouse at all, but rather an underground club run by local neo-Nazis.

So, yeah, the blonde wig was starting to make more and more sense as a fashion choice.

It was unclear to me if the people who came to the club were aware of the white supremacist ties, but it *was* clear to me that not a single Black or Brown person was going in or coming out.

The club worked as my cover. Pretty girls in tight clothes almost always got access to a club. Once I was in, though, my job was to find a way into the back.

Poor little lost drunk girl was my persona if I was caught.

Would I likely have to endure some dickhead's hand on my ass and breath in my ear for a moment or two before I steered myself back into the crowd? Sure. But I'd been in worse situations.

I was hoping I didn't get caught early, though. Because it would make being in that same area a second time acting "lost" look super suspicious.

And my research had told me that there was no other way to get into the back room where I needed to be.

Funny thing about city planning was it was pretty damn easy to get your hands on blueprints for a building.

You take that information and mingle it with firsthand accounts of checking out said building, and you learn all sorts of things.

Like there was a room that had been closed off to the inside of the building at some point in the warehouse's history, accessible only by the abandoned loading dock. The reason for closing it off was unknown. But where there was, on the plans, a little ten-by-twelve room—perhaps a storage closet at one time—there was now... nothing. Nothing save for a crawl space accessed via one of those ladder systems that unfolds from the ceiling and would allow me to climb up into the ductwork that a trusted source told me would be sturdy enough to hold me.

"If you were even just twenty pounds heavier, I would advise it," he'd said, eyes moving over me. But not in a creepy way. Just appraising my frame. "They're sturdy things, lots of anchoring. Especially in industrial buildings like that. But as you go on, it will narrow, and you'll have no choice but to exit through it, or slowly back back out of it."

I'd thanked him for that.

But I wasn't planning on going far.

The room next to the closed off room was where I was heading. Not to exit down into.

Just to listen through.

That was why, in the other cup not hiding my phone, I had a little recording device.

I prayed that if they used a panel on me, and there was some static as it moved over my boobs, that the bouncer at the door was just stupid enough to believe it was the underwire of my bra.

Shaking the tension out of my shoulders, I walked down the street, leaving my car in its designated location so no one would be able to see it and trace it back to me.

Then I walked toward the line of the club, my stupid little wrist purse swinging with each step. It was full of my fake IDs. And cash. In case I needed to do the unthinkable and give these shitheads some of my money just to keep up my ruse.

I couldn't see past the two tall, willowy women in front of me until they were allowed in the club to a chorus of rave music as the door swung open and closed.

Then there he was.

The doorman.

Tall, shaved head, wearing all black.

With double-eight tattoos on one side of his neck, and double s's on the other. Not even trying to hide his hatred from the rest of the world.

"ID," he barked at me, like he had at the women before me. Likely so used to attractive women at his job that their appeal was all but lost on him as he took IDs and looked them over.

Why, I had no idea.

This place wasn't legit.

But, I guess, if there was one way to get the law on your ass, it was to over-serve someone underaged, and piss off their parents who had to stand by while they got their stomachs pumped.

"Alright," he said, handing it back as I took out the fifty, like everyone else did, and handed it to him.

I'd never wished so hard before that I had some convincing counterfeit cash as I did right then. Because handing him money felt a fuckuva lot like funding a terrorist organization.

But it had to be done, so I tried to push the thoughts away as I moved in the club, wincing at the sheer volume of the music, the way the electronic sounds seemed to pump through my veins and organs, immediately intensifying the feeling of anxiety that had already been pulsing through me.

The crowd was surprisingly big, and I found myself hoping that these people *didn't* know who owned this club, because the thought of this many people in my hometown area being that racist hurt my soul.

"Focus," I hissed to myself as bodies knocked into me from all sides as I moved through the crowd.

Aware that there were probably cameras somewhere in the building, I tried to put on a show. Wiggling my hips, shaking my ass, throwing my hands up in the air.

"Hey, baby," a voice called from behind me as hands grabbed my hips, yanking me backward by them until my ass was pressed up against his groin. And the guy had no shame, trying to grind me against his erection before I yanked away, putting a group of other people between us.

I was losing my sense of direction as the crowd pushed me around. That, along with the dark room illuminated only by the occasional eye-splittingly bright strobe lights, had me disoriented until, by pure fate alone, I found myself on the wall opposite the crowded bar.

There was a hall on this side.

Toward the left, it went toward the men's room. To the right, the women's.

There was a long line for the women's, as there always was at any bar or club, thanks to them only ever having two or three stalls while the men had ten or more urinals lining one side of the room, allowing more people in and out quickly.

Luckily, the men's line was nonexistent. Because that was the direction I needed to go in.

The lie if I was caught there was easy.

"The girls take too long!"

As if I planned to walk my ass into a men's room at a club by myself, chancing God-knew what because bad things often happened when you found yourself in a closed room with a bunch of drunk, strange men.

When that pack mentality kicked in, making monsters of men.

Just ten or so feet beyond the men's room, though, was another, shorter, hall that broke off toward the back of the building.

That was where I was going.

From there, two doors down, then into the abandoned loading dock.

I'd be completely vulnerable there, easy to spot, to know I was where I wasn't supposed to be.

If anyone was paying attention to that area, I would be seen.

The job would be lost.

And, likely, some of my respect in this very niche world I worked inside of.

Heart hammering so hard I no longer heard the music, I wrenched open the door, then rushed in, closing it behind me, and all but running across the long, open space.

I had no idea how long I had, or what it would entail to get myself into the ductwork in the first place, so I needed to hurry.

The floor made my heels click far too loudly, clomping like the sound of my heart in my ears, making me sure that someone was going to hear it, and come to get me.

But no one came.

And the access to the storage room was where I knew it was supposed to be.

The door to access it was heavy and loud, but I tried to convince myself that it wasn't something anyone but me would hear, not with the racket going on in the club.

The space I moved into was dark, having no source of outside light, and any that had been inside had long since burned out.

I felt my way around the space, only stopping when I felt for the tab in the ceiling, then pulling the creaky ladder down inch by inch, trying to keep it as quiet as possible.

I kept my shoes on as I made my way up, only removing them at the very top, not wanting them to make any noise as I got into the ducts.

Taking slow, deep breaths to steady myself, I crawled across some narrow, slippery metal beams before I came to what I was seeking. The end of the elbow of the ductwork, the end that my friend assured me would pull off so HVAC guys could access the inside if they needed to.

With that, I pulled it off, the metal biting into my fingertips, then I climbed in, surprised how tight the space was when it looked so huge.

My friend had failed to warn me of something else about the ducts.

That the metal was unpredictably sharp in places, cutting into my hands and legs as I crawled, making me have to press my lips together to keep from crying out as I felt the blood start to trickle down my skin, likely mingling with all sorts of nasty shit accumulated in the ductwork throughout the years.

Thankfully, I'd had a recent tetanus shot.

But I was going to need to clean the shit out of my wounds to avoid infection.

I'd only crawled maybe a yard or so when I heard

it.

The sound of male voices.

Surprisingly close, given how high the ceilings were.

But the ductwork had lots of little vents into each room, so that was likely why the voices carried.

Holding my breath, I climbed as close as I dared to their sounds, then reached for my recording device, and turning it on as I held it to the vent.

My heartbeat was thrumming so hard in my ears that I honestly didn't hear a fucking thing they were saying. I didn't need to. Nor did I *want* to. I couldn't imagine these assholes would be saying anything I wanted to hear. I just needed to get as much of a recording as possible, then get my ass safely back out of this place.

That was it.

The job would be done.

It wouldn't be my fault if the client didn't get anything useful out of the recording. That wasn't the agreement.

I don't know how long I sat there, arm outstretched, muscle starting to twitch with the strain.

My wounds on my hands and legs had their own pulse now, a throbbing sensation that paired with the burning of open, dirty cuts.

It would all be worth it, I had to remind myself.

Especially if my client was going to make a move on these guys because of the information I'd gotten for him.

When the male voices drifted off, I turned off the device, tucking it safely away.

I waited, wanting to be sure no one was left behind, possibly hearing me as I started to move again, this time more clumsily than before, since I was backing up, unable to see where I was going, or what was behind me.

I knocked over one of my shoes at the end of the ductwork, making my pulse shoot into overdrive as I waited, making sure no one heard and came running.

I didn't slip them back on, just grabbed one in my hand and one tucked under my chin, and felt backward for the steps to the ladder.

Then I moved down them, small bits of the tension leaving me as I went.

The ductwork was the scariest part for me going in. And it was done. The material I was hired to collect was secured.

Now?

Now I just needed to make an exit.

Keep myself calm and collected until I was sure I wasn't followed, then drive.

The drive would calm my nerves, get my head on straight. Then I could go back to the office, clue in Josie, clean up, and go home.

It would all just be an ugly memory in a few days.

I slipped my feet back into my shoes in the little storage room, not even bothering to put the ladder back up, not wanting to chance the noise again now that I was so close to being done with this awful job.

I took all of ten seconds to try to yank my dress down to wipe some of the blood off my legs, then rubbed my arms against the black material that would hide the stains as well, before making my way back toward the loading dock.

I was rushing.

Ready to be done.

And, therefore, not paying attention.

Careless.

But I didn't know that.

Not until I felt hands reach out to grab me, pulling me up right off my feet, and slamming me against the unyielding steel walls of the loading dock, my head hitting it so hard that my vision swam for a second.

"Where the fuck you think you're going?" he snarled as one of his hands released me, only to shoot out and close around my throat. Not enough to knock me out, just enough to be really fucking painful as my head started to feel light, and my thoughts a little sluggish.

I had just remembered my bracelet when I felt his other hand slam into my face, the pain exploding across my cheekbone, then the whole side of my face.

I'd been hit before.

Mostly teenage skirmishes.

But that was nothing compared to a big, grown-ass man using all his strength against you.

He was a big man, too. Just as tall and wide as the security guard out front, but with wider hands.

"The fuck you think you're doing in here, bitch?" he snarled, landing another fist, but this one lower, catching me in the gut hard enough to knock the wind out of me, and make me want to fold forward to ease the ache, but it was impossible with his hand still around my throat.

"Why don't you tell me what you were doing in

here?" he asked, but he didn't even give me a chance to feed him a lie, because his fist was landing another blow to my face, making my teeth knock together, the pain blinding for a moment.

Focus.

I needed to focus.

The bracelet.

Thank *God* I had thought to put on the bracelet.

My attacker was busy snarling something at me as he held his fist in my face, threatening, like he was waiting for me to give him a reason to hit me again.

I tried to keep the movements of my hands small as I worked the clasp free on the chain, then spread it between my hands, wrapping its length around my palms, then pulling it tight.

Before I could raise them, though, there was another punch. I managed to yank my head to the side just enough for it to graze my jaw instead of my already-battered cheek.

There was no time even to process that new pain as I yanked my arms up between his, and pressed the chain as hard as I could into his throat.

It wasn't a good enough angle to choke him out. He could easily move away, out of reach.

But that didn't matter.

What mattered was that it caught him off guard.

That was a feat I managed, shocking him enough to drop his hand from my throat.

Without that pinning me to the wall, I didn't pause, didn't try to defend myself—because there was no defense against an attacker this much bigger than me —I just turned and ran.

I got maybe six or seven feet before a hand shoved out hard, sending me hurtling forward, my feet wobbling in my unsteady heels, making it impossible to right myself before I was falling forward.

I landed hard on hands and knees, the pain ratcheting up to my shoulders and hips at the impact.

There was no time to scramble up, because he was right on me, his booted foot striking out, making contact again with my stomach, sending me flying over onto my back.

On the ground was the worst place to be. There were too many ways a woman could be overpowered and violated.

But it was also the only way for me to reach into my shoe, and grab something to defend myself with.

My hand closed around the petite knife. It wasn't much. A glorified nail file in size. But strong and very pointed.

I resisted the urge to hold it in the natural way, gripping the handle instead fully in my fist with just the very tip sticking out of the pinky side of my hand.

"The fuck you think you're—" he started as he leaned over me.

Refusing to think, I struck outward, feeling the resistance as the knife met flesh and muscle and maybe bone. I had no idea.

All I knew was he howled hard.

I didn't try to pull it out or strike again.

I didn't even stop to see where I'd stabbed him.

I scrambled back, gained my feet, and fucking ran.

My heels slammed against the ground as I flew back toward the door that led to the hall, wrenched it open, saying a silent prayer that more assholes weren't in wait, and flew into the area by the bathrooms.

Maybe people looked.

Maybe they gasped at the sight of me.

I had no idea.

I was blinded with my need to get away.

And the only way I could do that was to disappear into the crowd of bodies in the club.

I did, pushing through as quickly as I could, frustrated whimpers escaping me as the people slowed me down.

What felt like forever later, but was likely less than a minute or two, I burst through the back of the crowd, and made a mad dash to the door.

I shouldered someone so hard coming in the door that they went flying, landing hard on their ass, getting immediate attention, drawing it away from me as I ran.

Down the alley between buildings, losing the wig because this was not a clean getaway, and anything that could easily identify me was worse than them seeing my actual hair color for just a moment.

My thighs felt like they were wobbling from the adrenaline as I flew behind a line of dumpsters before emerging on the street where my car was parked, hidden slightly behind a big van.

I felt tears sting my eyes as I neared it, even as I heard raised, angry male voices, likely spreading out to try to find me.

I bleeped my locks, hauled myself in, turned the engine, and fucking floored it.

I was a blur in seconds, too fast for anyone to make out the license plate or even the model of my car. Not that the plate mattered. I always had a dummy one on it just in case.

I knew speeding was a bad move in a party town teeming with police, but my entire body was starting to tremble, and I was worried I would lose complete control of myself before I was safely away.

"Focus, focus," I told myself, blinking the useless tears out of my eyes as I weaved in and out of traffic, up and down streets, trying to make sure I had no tail, but cutting it shorter than I normally would have when the shaking started to become almost violent.

I parked around the corner from work, pausing just to pull off the dummy plates, then rushing on unsteady legs toward the office, unlocking it, moving inside, locking the door again, then collapsing down on the floor just inside the entrance.

"Fuck fuck fuck," I hissed, pressing the heels of my filthy hands to my eyes. Like the pressure alone could keep the wetness in. But it was useless. The tears flowed down my cheeks as I curled into myself, ignoring the pain it caused, hugging my legs to my chest, trying to hold myself together as my nervous system seemed bent on falling apart.

I couldn't tell you how long I sat there, shaking, crying, completely losing my shit.

But, eventually, I climbed my ass back up off that floor, took myself into the bathroom where I finally got a look at myself.

The makeup was smeared all over my face.

But as I carefully removed that, I could see the

beginnings of the bruises. On my jaw, cheek, a big ring around my eye.

And my throat.

The outline of a man's fingers was forming.

I dapped a little antiseptic spray on my lip that had a small split, then got to work removing the tattoo covering makeup from my arms, so I could clean the wounds on them and my legs from the jagged metal of the air duct.

Then and only then did I go back out into the office, finding my phone in my bag, and texting a Josie I know was sitting at home, worried sick.

I didn't lie to her.

I didn't say it went well.

I just gave her all I could.

It's done.

Then I went home to nurse my wounds in private. Where no one could see me.

Until, of course, there was a knock at my door the next evening.

Chapter Fifteen

Cato

I tried to tell myself I was only heading in that direction because I was in the area.

I mean, I was.

Levee wanted to go visit his nasty-ass uncle, and I'd come along for moral support. But as usual, the old man kicked me out, so I had time to myself while Levee dealt with the dickhead who would do nothing but berate Levee as he tried to help.

I mean, yeah, damnit, alright.

I'd only tagged along because it would put me in the area. And being in the area gave me an excuse to go drop in to see her at work without it seeming like I was fucking stalking her because she wasn't answering me.

Since I hadn't been doing much sleeping the night before, I'd managed to overthink myself into believing she was pushing me away, that she was trying to break shit off without having to actually do it.

But... fuck that.

If she wanted out, I wanted her to say it to my face. No easy way out.

Because I was sure that if we were face-to-face, it would be harder for her to lie to herself about not wanting me.

She did.

She was just running scared.

If I had a chance to show her that there was nothing she needed to run from, I was going to take advantage of it.

Even if it bruised my pride a bit to have to do so.

I parked my bike around the corner from her work, hoping she wouldn't spook and lock the place up when she heard the rumble, and just assumed it was someone passing by.

Anticipation wobbled around in my stomach as I grabbed the handle of the door and made my way inside.

To find Josie sitting at her desk in a bright yellow sundress, a book in her hand, and the cat sitting at the edge of her desk, slowly sticking his paw in and out, like he was waiting for her to tell him not to knock over her pen cup.

But she wasn't paying him any attention.

Which also seemed to piss him off, so he swatted at it, and the clatter had Josie nearly jumping out of her skin.

"Binxy!" she said, sighing.

But it was then that Binx saw me in the doorway, greeting me with a hiss that revealed his pointy teeth.

Josie's brows pinched, but she followed his line of sight, jolting a bit when she saw me looming there inside the door.

"Sorry," I said, holding up a hand to her. "Didn't mean to scare you."

"Hey, Cato," she said, giving me a small smile as I moved inside.

"I got it," I told her, going toward the end of the

desk, and gathering her scattered pens and cup, then putting them on the other side of the desk, away from the grumpy-ass cat.

"Thank you," she said, giving me a shy smile.

"Is Rynn around?" I asked, glancing around like there was anywhere she could be hiding in the small office.

"Ah, no, she... she said she was taking today off," Josie said. "You... haven't heard from her?" she asked.

Why did that question seem so loaded?

Did she know something about the situation with me and Rynn that I didn't? She was Rynn's only friend.

"No, she hasn't answered my texts. Or calls," I admitted, shaking my head. "Honestly, I thought she was giving me the brush off. But I wanted her to do it to my face if that was the case."

"I... I don't think that's it," Josie said, hedging. Something was going on here, but she didn't want to tell me.

"What's going on, Josie?" I asked, not liking how tense she was, how her fingers were fidgeting, fanning the pages of her book over and over.

"She had a job last night. And I'm worried about her," she admitted.

"Have you checked on her?"

"I asked if she wanted me to drop off some lunch for her a while ago, but she just sent me back a kind of curt *No*. It's just... it's not like her. I mean... Rynn doesn't turn down food."

"Give me her address," I demanded, trying to keep my voice soft even if anxiety was working its way up my spine, making me tense. "Give it to me, or I will look it up myself. But I'm going over there to check on her."

That seemed to change something in her. Maybe the desperate, but hard edge to my words. My determination to make sure she was okay.

"Okay," she said, rattling off an address. "She... she likes Big Gulps of soda," she said, giving me a nod.

"Got it," I agreed, nodding. "If you give me your number, I will text you what I find out," I told her.

She jumped on that, rattling it off.

"Hey, Cato," she called as I got to the door.

"Yeah?" I asked, turning back.

"You're really good for her," she said, giving me a small smile.

"I really like her," I admitted.

Then I was off, getting on my bike, and taking the short ride toward her building, a tall apartment complex, all white walls and big panes of glass reflecting the lights of the city back at me.

I did stop at the convenience store at the corner, grabbing her drink and some of that damn cheddar popcorn, then making my way into her building.

It struck me again how little I knew about her work, about how she made her money. But, clearly, she made a lot of it. Because this place was fucking lush. Even the smallest apartments had to be going for a couple grand a month. And Rynn was up in one of the two penthouses.

I rode the elevator up, listening to the classical music on the speaker as I went, surprised by how nervous I was to show up at her door.

What if she didn't answer?

Did I force my way in?

To check on her? To make sure she was alright?

Especially if Josie was worried about her. Josie who *did* know what the nature of her job was, what dangers were involved, what kind of trouble Rynn could have gotten into.

It could be bad.

And if she needed some sort of help, we had to get that for her.

I walked down the hallway between the two penthouse apartments, both of them managing to have ocean views thanks to the way they were laid out, and found my way to Rynn's, smirking down at her welcome mat. Black with white writing that said *There's no reason for you to be here.*

Taking a deep breath, I knocked on the white door. Once. Twice. Three times.

Then a fourth.

Why the fuck wasn't she answering?

Casting a glance toward the neighbor's door, I started to reach in my wallet.

I'd been carrying a small lock pick set since I was a kid. I was decent enough at it. Though who knew what other kinds of locks she might have on a door in this fancy-ass apartment building.

I listened, figuring I would give her another minute to come. She could be sleeping or in the bathroom or something. But when she didn't come, I found the picks, put the drink and popcorn down, and got to work.

It gave, and swung slightly open, no extra locks to worry about.

I was just standing back up from grabbing her drink and popcorn when I saw it.

A slash of blood on the inner molding of the door.

"Fuck," I hissed, moving inside.

While, yes, the building itself might have been white and bright and sunny, it came as no surprise to me that Josie's apartment itself was more like her office.

Dark.

Moody.

The walls themselves were painted a forest green so deep that it was almost black. The artwork over the long sectional that seemed to match the one in her office were in big, gold frames, and were prints of what looked like haunted houses, old, dilapidated insane asylums, somber looking women in gowns, and flower arrangements.

There were french doors out onto a balcony overlooking the water, and a small dining table that seemed unused, as it was covered in unopened delivery boxes.

To the other side of the sprawling common space was the kitchen.

I imagine, when she moved in, the thing had been all white. That was what was trendy in places like that.

But it didn't suit Rynn.

It didn't matter that she didn't cook.

She still wanted it to match her personal preferences.

The cabinets themselves were a another shade so dark that it was almost black, but this time it was an umber brown. There were gold cabinet pulls, exposed upper cabinets showing off a dark collection of dinnerware, and a shiny, dark green tile backsplash. The countertops were a deep gray color.

On the center of the island was a pitcher full of black roses that were quickly wilting, a few petals scattered around the counter.

I put her drink and popcorn down on that island as I moved toward the hallway, my pulse quickening now that I knew that whatever had gone down had involved bloodshed.

Hers.

I had no idea how it happened.

But if a person was involved in that bleeding? Yeah, they were going to fucking pay for it.

My blood was pounding in my ears, making it impossible to hear anything over it as I moved down the hall, passing an empty bedroom, save for several cat trees and some intricate system on the walls for the cats to use as a jungle gym.

One of said cats, another black one, was lying upside down on one of the tree stands, batting lazily at a mouse-shaped toy above her head.

The other cat was missing.

I couldn't help but wonder if it was like Binx, lying in wait, ready to scratch a chunk of me out.

There was a half bath next.

Then, finally, the primary bedroom.

The door was mostly closed, but I pushed it open.

This room, this was all darkness.

Blackness.

Black being the only color in the space. The walls, the furniture, the big headboard, the chandelier over the bed, the bedding itself.

The only spot of light in the room was a pale shoulder sticking out of the covers.

I froze, watching her for a second, my own breath caught in my chest until I saw her body moving slowly, but steadily, in her sleep.

Asleep.

Not dead.

Not so terribly injured that she was on the brink of death.

I would like to say I relaxed, but I didn't.

Just because she wasn't dying didn't mean she was okay.

If she was okay, she would have assured Josie that she was. She would have accepted her friend's offer to bring her some food.

Something was wrong.

"Rynn," I called, voice low, figuring maybe I could slowly ease her toward consciousness. "Rynn," I tried again, getting closer to the bed. "Baby, wake up," I demanded more firmly. "Rynn," I tried, louder, this time reaching out to touch her shoulder.

That was the wrong move.

She snapped awake, moving almost in a blur she was so fast.

Clearly, she was on high alert, because no one moved like that unless shit had gone down.

One second, she was asleep.

The next, she was swinging a knife at me.

My own hand shot out, grabbing her wrist just before it could slice my arm, and holding it in a firm grip.

"Baby…" I started, then I actually got a look at her.

"Baby, what the fuck happened?" I asked, voice tight.

Josie was right.

Something was definitely not fucking okay.

Whatever "job" she'd been on had gone sideways.

Because someone had used her face as a punching bag. She was swollen and bruised, purple and blue mottling her jaw and cheek, and encircling her eye.

There was a small slit in her lip.

Below that, the bruises on her neck told a very clear fucking story. Someone had strangled her.

Mother fucker.

Unable to stop myself, I reached out with my free hand, whipping the blankets off of her.

I don't know what the fuck happened, but there were bruises on her knees and lacerations all over her arms and legs.

"Cato?" she asked, voice so small that I barely even heard it.

As quiet as it was, though, I could tell from the wince on her face that it hurt.

I carefully pulled the knife from her hand, setting it on the nightstand.

"Josie sent me," I told her. "We were both worried about you."

"I'm fine," she insisted, voice like gravel.

"You're not fine," I said.

She was going to be difficult about this. It was her

nature. And I had to roll with that.

"Hold on. I got you a drink," I told her. "The cold might help that throat," I added, turning and going into the hall to grab the soda, but not before I shot a text to a worried Josie.

She was beat up on this job.

- Is she okay?

She's okay, but it's rough. I'll update you later.

I made my way back to the bedroom to find her sitting up against the headboard, a hand to her throat, a far-away, tortured look in her eyes.

"If this goes down like glass, I can make you something warm instead," I told her, handing her the Big Gulp as I kicked out of my shoes, and made my way around the bed.

"What are you doing?" she asked, wincing again with the effort to speak.

"Getting in bed with you," I told her, doing just that as she took a sip of her drink, paused, then took another.

"Why?"

"Because you need someone, but you're such a fucking stubborn ass that you won't admit that. So I am just going to sit here and be there for you until are ready to talk. Does that TV work?" I asked, pointing across the room to her black dresser with its black, oversized frame.

Deciding not to fight me, because whether she

liked it or not, she did need someone.

So she reached over for the remote. The twisting had her taking a sharp intake of breath.

There were other injuries.

I wanted to see them all, to tell her if she needed to go see someone. Maybe Seeley's girl, Ama, if she wouldn't go to a hospital. But I needed to go slow with her.

"Thanks," I said, tone calm, turning on the TV and flicking through the channels, settling on a sitcom that was light and easy, hoping it would break up the heavy mood in the room.

"I'm fine," she insisted again, and I was wondering if she was trying to convince me or herself.

"Of course you are," I agreed, nodding.

She might have been beat down and bruised, but this was Rynn. She was okay. Or she would be after she healed up.

"I had a job," she told me what felt like an eternity later. "It... didn't go how I planned. And I planned a lot," she said, then was silent for a minute, sipping the drink.

I had been choked out once in my life. And I distinctly remembered the next day, how swallowing my spit was torture, let alone speaking.

"Sometimes it doesn't matter how much you plan, or how good you are. Shit just goes sideways."

"Yeah," she said, nodding, eyes far off for a moment, then shaking her head like she was trying to break the thoughts free.

"Can I ask you something?" I asked.

"Okay."

"Did you treat those cuts?" I asked, waving toward her legs.

"Yes."

"Can I treat them again?" I asked. "They're looking a little puffy."

"I can—" she started.

"Hey, I asked if I could," I repeated.

"Okay," she relented.

"In the primary bathroom or the hall one?" I asked, pointing each way.

"This one."

"Alright."

With that, I climbed off the bed, making my way into the bathroom.

More of the same dark colors.

Even the tile in the shower stall and the soaking tub itself.

Opening the storage cabinet, I found a plastic container jammed full of first aid supplies, making me wonder yet again what the fuck this woman did for a living that had her so stocked up on bandages, antiseptic, little plastic tiles of sealed saline, butterfly sutures, ointments and salves, and even a fucking kit to do her own stitches.

I gathered what I needed, washed my hands, and made my way back to the bed, sitting at her feet, spreading towels, and getting to work cleaning the wounds with the saline, then letting them dry before slathering on some triple antibiotic, then figuring out how to put bandage them without the adhesive touching the other cuts.

I decided on gauze, then wrapping the legs with

186

some of the cohesive bandage wrap to wrap up her entire legs and arms.

I felt Rynn's gaze on me the whole time, but said nothing, just let her think through whatever was going on in her head.

Finished, I put everything on the nightstand, knowing this would need to be repeated again in the morning.

"How about some ice for your face?" I asked, looking up at her. It took actual work to keep my jaw slack and my eyes from slitting when I looked up at her pretty face all battered like that.

There would be a time and a place for my anger. This wasn't it.

"Okay," she agreed.

"Want anything else while I'm out there? Something to eat? I know it will be a bitch to choke anything down, but I could pick up some ice cream."

"You don't hav—"

"What kind of ice cream do you want, baby?" I cut her off.

"Vanilla bean. Or caramel. Or…strawberry."

"Vanilla, caramel, and strawberry it is," I agreed. "Give me twenty. Don't lock the door on me. It was a pain in the ass to have to pick it," I added, leaning over her to press a kiss to the top of her head, then making my way out.

I paused just outside her building, head tipped back, eyes closed, taking a few deep breaths.

Then I reached for my phone, calling Josie.

"Is she okay?" she answered before a full ring could even finish. Her voice was raised and clipped.

"She's… recovering. I don't think she needs to see a doctor. But she's rough, Josie."

"Tell me," she demanded.

"Black eye, bruised cheek and jaw. Someone strangled her, she's got a finger necklace of bruises…"

"Oh, my God," Josie gasped.

"There are cuts all up and down her legs. I treated those. They were looking gnarly. Any idea if she's had a tetanus shot recently?"

"Yeah, a couple years ago."

"Good. She's got bruised hands and knees. And there's something wrong with her stomach or rib area, but I haven't pressed her on that yet. But that would be the thing I'm most worried about. A broken rib or something like that. So I will have her let me look eventually."

"How is she… you know… emotionally?" Josie asked.

"A little withdrawn, which freaks me the fuck out," I admitted. "I want her to open up to me, but I'm trying not to force it. I'm just popping out to pick her up some ice cream. Getting strangled makes your throat hurt like a motherfucker."

"She likes ice pops too. And slushies."

"What kind?" I asked, ready to fill her oversized freezer with everything I could get my hands on that she liked.

"You know those, like, watermelon ice pop things you could get from the ice cream man?"

"Yeah."

"She likes those. And, if they have them, the baseball mitt ones. There is an off-brand that makes those now since I don't think you can buy them in stores. She likes orange cream pops and ice cream sandwiches, but not the cones and not the red, white, and blue pops."

"You're a wealth of Rynn knowledge," I said, feeling my lips curve up slightly.

"She doesn't open up easily. Except about food," Josie admitted. "As for slushies, she likes them all. But she usually mixes the fruit ones in layers. Should I come and check on her?" she asked.

"I think one person is all she can take right now, but I will text you in the morning if I think she is up for more company. She can't really even talk much right now, so it would just be sitting in awkward silence."

"Okay. I understand. If she asks, tell her I am taking care of Binxy and the office."

"Oh, speaking of cats. Is there anything I should be picking up for the ones at her place?" I asked.

"She has everything on auto delivery. So if you can't find something, it's probably in that mound of boxes she always has piling up."

"Okay. Thanks again, Josie. I promise I'll update you as I know more."

I made my way back to the convenience store, and was stocking up on just about every ice cream concoction known to mankind when my phone started to ring.

Levee.

Shit.

I'd forgotten about him.

"Hey, man. Where you at?"

"Fuck, man, I forgot. Something came up with Rynn. It's… she got beat up, man," I admitted.

"She… what? By who?" he asked, voice getting tight, pissed off. Because he liked Rynn. She was part of our world now. And also just on principle. It was hard to find someone who enjoyed women quite as much as Levee did. He took it personally when someone put their hands on *any* of them.

"I don't know the details yet. Seems to be something with her work, but she was choked out, so she can't talk much yet."

"Fuck, man. Okay. You need anything from me?"

"No. Not yet anyway. I will let you know when I know more, though."

"Yeah. You know me. I'll ride if we have a mission."

He would, too.

Even though Levee didn't love the high-stakes, adrenaline-fueled parts of the job as much as I did, he was ready and capable of handling any situation that came at us.

"Thanks, Lev. I'll let you know."

By the time I made it back to the apartment, Rynn was out of bed and in the kitchen, most of the apartment lights on, illuminating every single corner of the room. The way someone would want when some bad shit had gone down, and they suddenly found themselves jumping at shadows.

One of her black cats was standing on the counter, waiting for her to finish putting some wet food into a fancy-ass crown-shaped bowl.

The other cat was already eating out of hers.

"Hey," I said, not wanting to startle her.

"Hey," she replied, voice barely carrying across the expansive space. "Wow," she said, eyes widening as she caught sight of all of the bags I was carrying.

"Think I bought out the frozen dessert section," I admitted. "Also picked up some yogurt and applesauce. Gotta have something other than ice cream, but I know the softer shit is better right now," I added, taking it all out of the bags, so she could see the options.

"You talked to Josie," she said.

It wasn't a question.

"Yeah. She's worried about you. I just wanted to tell her you were okay. And she suggested a few things. Here," I said, passing her the slushie. "Blue raspberry, raspberry, and cherry. In layers," I added, watching as her lips turned slightly up at the corners. Not a smile. But close.

"We hanging out here, or going back to bed?" I asked.

"You don't have to stay," she said, using the scoop end of the spoon to taste her slushie since I was pretty sure sucking on a straw would be pretty miserable.

"I'm staying. Stop making a big deal out of it," I said, pulling open drawers until I found the utensil one, then handing her a spoon. "It'll all turn to juice before you can eat it all with that straw."

"Why are you being so nice?" she asked, gaze cast down.

"Would you like it better if I was being an asshole right now?" I shot back.

"Maybe," she admitted, this time giving me a small

smile.

"Know what I think?" I asked.

"What?"

"I think you aren't used to anyone wanting to take care of you, so me being here is making you a little emotional. Oh, stop," I said, rolling my eyes when she opened her mouth to object. Which was pointless. Because even mentioning her emotions had her eyes looking suddenly glassy.

"Listen," I said, ducking down to keep her gaze. "I want to be here. Helping you isn't a burden. And it's perfectly normal to be a little fucking upset about what happened to you."

I had a feeling that those were things no one had ever said to her before. What with her selfish, loon of a mother and her absent father. Then her complete lack of a close friend group or, it seemed, relationships.

"Stop," she demanded as a single tear slid free of her lashes and slipped down her cheek.

"Stop giving a shit about you?" I asked, reaching out to catch the tear. "No, baby. That's not gonna fucking happen. So you might as well get used to it. And for the record, this," I said, snagging another tear with the side of my finger, "doesn't bother me. So you don't gotta bottle it all up."

That seemed to be what she needed to hear.

Because the second she did, her lower lip wobbled, and the dams broke, sending water pouring down her cheeks.

Her hands went up, pressing into her eyes like she could stem the flow even as I moved around the counter, sidestepping a eating cat, and reaching to pull her against my chest.

"I don't cry," she insisted on a hitching voice.

"Of course not," I agreed, running my hand through her hair as she, in fact, cried into my chest. "You're just... washing your eyes," I added, getting a snorting sound out of her before another silent sob racked her body.

Neither of us said anything. We just stood there as she let all the fear and uncertainty and grief work its way through her system.

Her arms went around me after, squeezing hard.

"Baby, can I look at your stomach?" I asked after a couple moments passed. "I'm worried about your ribs," I admitted as her arms slowly slid from my back.

She said nothing, but she moved back, wiping her eyes, then just... waiting.

Taking the cue, I lifted up the hem of her tank top to just under her breasts.

The skin of her stomach was discolored, mottled with shades of blue, purple, green, and yellow. But not near her ribs. More centered.

Like someone kicked her in the stomach.

My jaw ached, reminding me I needed to relax it as my hand moved out, prodding as gently as I could around her organs, wanting to make sure they weren't tender.

You have a lot going on in your abdomen. Liver, spleen, pancreas, bladder, your intestines themselves. All of 'em could be injured following a hard blow to the stomach.

There wasn't any swelling or hardness around. But

I was still a little worried about the whole area. A hard kick from a shoe-clad foot of a grown man could definitely do damage.

"Any chance I could convince you to see a friend of mine tomorrow to get an ultrasound done of this?" I asked, teasing my fingers gently over the bruising.

"A friend?" she asked.

"Seeley's girl, Ama, she's a doctor. Runs a clinic not far away. She will see you without paperwork or questions. Just to be sure. This is the only thing we really need to worry about."

"Just an ultrasound?"

"Maybe some bloodwork," I added.

"Okay," she relented, likely just as concerned about it as I was. Internal bleeding was nothing to fuck with.

"Okay. Good. I will shoot her a text, and we will probably head over before the clinic opens in the morning."

"Okay," she agreed, nodding, and taking her slushie over to the couch.

I quickly put the cold stuff away, then walked into the bedroom to call Ama instead of text.

"Hey, is she okay?" Ama asked.

The grapevine worked fast in our wold. Levee to Seeley, Seeley to Ama.

"I think so. But I wanted to see if I can get her in for an ultrasound of her abdomen tomorrow morning?"

"An ultrasound looking for a heartbeat, or…" she hedged.

"She's not pregnant," I said, shaking my head even though she couldn't see me. "She was clearly kicked in the stomach. I just want to make sure there's no damage."

"Yeah, of course. I mean, if anything looks off, she will need a CT. Maybe with contrast. But we can cross that bridge if we come to it."

"Thanks, Ama. Just one thing… she doesn't want to talk about it. But…" I stopped, sighing hard, not sure how to phrase it.

"But you're worried there might be other abuses she's endured," she said, and I was grateful for the careful way she worded that. Because I was having a hard time wrapping my mind around that possible scenario.

"Yeah."

"Okay. I've been there before, Cato," she said, voice sad. "I will see what she can tell me, but I have to remind you that I can't tell you about that. That's her place to decide."

"I know. I just want to make sure she has someone to talk to if that's the case," I agreed, stomach twisting at the idea that she'd been put through that on top of everything else.

"I will be at the clinic at six. We open at eight. Anytime before that will be fine."

"Great. Thanks, Ama. I really appreciate it."

With that, I hung up, and made my way back out to the living room where Rynn was curled up with a movie on the TV.

We didn't talk.

We watched movies.

She ate her slushie and ice cream, then we went to the bedroom. She passed out after taking an old pain pill she had in a bottle in her medical kit.

Eventually, I slept too.

Chapter Sixteen

Rynn

I thought it wasn't possible to feel worse than I had right after the beating took place.

I'd been so incredibly wrong about that.

The following day had been infinitely worse.

I couldn't move without my stomach screaming in objection. I couldn't so much as swallow my own spit without feeling like I was gargling glass. My legs and arms felt too sensitive and sore from the cuts.

And to top off that shit sandwich, I had a blinding migraine that made it impossible to do anything but try to sleep it off after taking one of the pills I'd gotten almost a year back after falling off a stupid fire escape and onto the corner of a dumpster, fucking up my shoulder, and landing in a brace for a few weeks.

That pill had to be why I hadn't heard Cato knocking. I wasn't a light or heavy sleeper. I was, you know, normal. I could sleep through some sounds—especially the repetitive shit like the garbage trucks knocking around the dumpsters on trash day, the car horns, the sirens, the loud sounds of the city—but always woke up to something off—a knock at the door, the buzzer, something falling in the apartment because the cats decided they wanted to jump on a shelf they weren't supposed to be on.

It wasn't like me to sleep through someone

knocking, then forcing their way into my house, into my room, calling my name, then touching me to wake me up.

And, yeah, I'd been sleeping with a knife.

In fact, that wasn't all I'd been sleeping with.

I had a knife under my hand on the mattress, a bottle of mace on my nightstand, a bat under the bed, and a couple of tools—hammers, screwdrivers, a mallet, shit that could do some damage—placed strategically around my apartment.

I wasn't normally paranoid. Not even after a job didn't go to plan.

But that had been close. Way, way too close. As I replayed it over and over in my head, I saw all the ways that I could have been hurt, abused, violated, before someone finally decided to put me out of my misery, and dump my body somewhere.

And I'd been face-to-face with the guy for a long time. Long enough that I was worried he saw through my wig and makeup. Or that I could have been followed.

I expected that Josie might show up eventually, sensing something was off because I never called out of work like I had. Especially when I still had to give the client the information I'd gotten for them.

I thought maybe she would show up herself.

I never anticipated her sending Cato.

Or even that he would come, that he would be looking for me when he hadn't heard from me.

Not only had he shown up, but he'd insisted on staying, he'd treated my wounds, he'd gone out to get me things I could eat with my sore throat.

He'd held me when I cried.

I thought I would die of mortification afterward, but somehow, he just... made it seem like it was no big deal.

As I drifted off to sleep with him still right there beside me, I was reasonably sure that I had fallen for him. I mean, the whole 'love' thing was new to me. So I couldn't be certain, but that warm, chocolate lava cake sensation was back, and stronger.

Which sure seemed a lot like the love they talked about in music and movies.

I woke up the next morning alone, thinking he was gone, that he'd had time to think it over, and he was done with me.

There was no accounting for the crushing sensation in my chest at the idea.

Just to distract myself from it, I went into the bathroom, brushing my teeth, and pulling my hair up.

It was as I was coming out that I heard voices.

Male voices.

I rushed toward the bed, grabbing my bat, and creeping down the hall toward the sound, ready to beat some white supremacist's brains in.

Only to find Cato standing in the doorway with Eddie on the other side.

"Afraid you're not quite up to playing baseball yet, baby," Cato said, proving the man had insane peripheral vision because he hadn't even looked over.

"Oh..." The air whooshed out of me as relief surged through my system.

Not, I had to admit to myself, because I wasn't being invaded. But because I hadn't been abandoned.

"Oh, my girl," Eddie said, shaking his head sadly. "You give me names and numbers..."

"Eddie was bringing you some food. Soft stuff that you can get down without too much effort," he said. "Since I can't cook for shit."

"Don't worry, honey, I'll make him learn," Eddie said, giving me a smile, but there was tension around his eyes.

"You want to come in?" I asked, wincing a bit at the effort it took to speak. I needed a drink to soothe it.

"No, no, mami, I am gonna go back and make breakfast for the guys. Got new people to impress," he said. "Feel better," he said before turning and leaving.

"You didn't have to make him do that," I said as I went to the fridge to grab a cold drink.

"I didn't. Levee must have been talking. Eddie shows his love with food."

"I'm starving," I admitted. Sure, I'd choked down some ice cream and icees the night before, but it hadn't exactly been sustenance.

"Yeah you need some real food. We have to make it to Ama's clinic before eight," he told me. "But we'll eat as soon as we're back. Do they cats need anything?" I asked.

"Cats just need food and a clean litter box."

"I'll clean it after... why not?" he asked when I shook my head.

"I splurged to get them those fancy-ass robot ones that clean themselves."

"No shit?" he asked, brows raised.

Were they each a thousand dollars a piece? Sure. But not having to constantly scoop litter was priceless to me.

Originally, one of them had been for Binx. But he'd been so enraged by its very existence that he'd gone to the bathroom on the floor next to it rather than go inside.

So, my girls each had their own in their little cat room.

"What're their names?" he asked as one of them shamelessly slammed her body against his legs and started to rub up on him. She never did that to me. Apparently, she had a thing for men. The little floozy.

"That one falling in love with you is Sabrina. That one is Wednesday," I explained, pointing my fork over toward where Wednesday was staring down a bird that had landed on the balcony railing outside of the sliding doors.

"Why all black cats?" he asked.

"No one wants them," I explained. "And they're black," I added, waving around my apartment.

"Solid point," he agreed before we started getting ready to get going.

Ama's clinic was in the area where Cato and his friends had grown up. I'd passed it a million times, but it had clearly gotten a major upgrade recently.

Everything inside and out seemed new and state-of-the-art.

It was empty, though, save for the male nurse and a pretty brunette woman whose name tag said "Call me Ama."

"I'll take it from here, Cato," Ama told him, giving him a small smile as she led me back to an exam room.

"How are you feeling?" she asked as she rolled an

ultrasound machine over toward me.

"My throat is really my biggest complaint. Cato is worried about my legs, arms, and stomach, though."

"Can I take a look at your arms and legs?" she asked, motioning toward the wrap holding the gauze in place.

"Sure," I agreed, sitting back on the angled bed.

She put on gloves them unwrapped one of my legs, then the other, checking out the scratches.

"These look pretty good," she said. "Whatever you've been putting on is working. But I will redress it all, so you don't get anything in them on the way home. In another two or three days, you should be all closed up and won't need the bandages."

She got to work mostly in silence before she finally broke it.

"Hey, Rynn?"

"Yeah?"

"If something happened to you that you want to talk about, or want me to check out for you..." she said, letting the implications hang. "Or if you need some morning-after pills or a full STI panel run..."

She was worried I'd been raped.

Which, I assumed, Cato was worried about too, though he'd been delicate enough not to bring it up, leaving it to a professional—and a woman—to do so instead.

"I wasn't raped," I told her. "I mean... I think if I hadn't gotten away when I did, that was absolutely going to happen," I admitted, my worst fears spoken aloud for the first time. "But it didn't get that far."

"Okay. Well, I'm glad for your sake that is true.

Now, a tetanus…"

"I'm all good on that front," I assured her.

"Great. Then we can get right to this," she said, cleaning up her mess, then coming back to sit on her rolling stool as she reached to roll up my shirt.

She did the same sort of prodding Cato had done the night before. "I still want to do the ultrasound, but I'm not too worried about this," she told me even as she grabbed the gel, and squeezed a cold glob onto my skin before grabbing the wand to start looking around.

"You know, when Cato first mentioned you needing an ultrasound, I thought you might be pregnant," she admitted.

I expected to recoil from those words.

I didn't want kids.

Right?

I mean, I had nothing against kids.

But I just never saw them in my future.

That said, I'd also never seen a partner in my future. And if I didn't see a husband, why would I see kids?

The possibility was hanging in the air right then, though. Intriguing. Almost… tempting. But requiring a lot more thought to wrap my head around.

"I've been on the Pill since I was fifteen," I admitted. "No babies for me. Anytime soon," I tacked on at the end where I previously never would have.

"You're still young if you decide," she said, shrugging as she moved the wand around. "Okay. I feel pretty confident saying this looks okay. I am going to suggest a blood test. Just to test your hemoglobin and platelet levels as well as your liver enzymes. If you were bleeding anywhere, they would be lower than usual. It's just a good, final precaution to ease everyone's worries.

"I'd also like to run a quick pregnancy test. Just to be sure. It's a test I always run just to be sure."

"Okay," I agreed, nodding.

She left the room for a minute, coming back to draw my blood, to collect the sample for the pregnancy test, then leaving again.

When she came in the last time, she told me that the pregnancy test, as anticipated, was negative. Then she produced a bottle of liquid.

"I don't know for sure if this will work," she said, holding up the bottle of spray meant for sore throats.

"Girls in high school used to use that to suppress their gag reflexes to give head," I said, getting a laugh out of Ama.

"Yeah," she agreed, nodding. "Which was part of the reason I brought it in. If it helps that, it might help your throat. Just so you can eat and talk normally while you heal. But try not to use it excessively."

I gave it a try, making a face at the taste, but slowly but surely, a welcome numbness started to spread.

"All good news," Ama told a worried Cato who popped up out of his seat as soon as we walked out.

"I'm not pregnant!" I announced, getting a chuckle from Ama but a wide-eyed look from Cato.

"Was there... was there some concern about that?" he asked.

"Don't worry. I pop my Pill with my morning coffee every day. No little Catos anytime soon," I said, watching his eyes warm as I realized what the hell I'd just said.

Anytime soon?

God.

What was wrong with me?

"Ama gave me blowjob spray," I blurted out, trying to change the topic quickly.

"Blowjob spray," he repeated, lips twitching.

"To numb my throat," I explained.

"Right. Right," he said, shaking his head, looking a little flustered. Considering how much fucking we'd done, and how filthy his mouth was, it was kind of endearing to see him look uncomfortable about the topic of head.

Everyone said their goodbyes, and we climbed back into my car that we'd taken so it wasn't so rough on my sore stomach with all the bumps and potholes.

"I wasn't raped," I told him as we drove in silence. Cato's gaze cut to me. "I know you were worried about that."

"For the record, I was worried for you."

"Why would you need to clarify that?" I asked, shaking my head.

"Knew this asshole years back who had a girlfriend who was jumped and raped on her way home from work. He told her that he felt like she cheated on him. Fucking broke that girls heart to pieces saying that shit. Just wanted to make sure it was clear I wasn't like him."

"I wouldn't have thought that of you," I said, my own heart aching for that poor girl. And any other woman who dealt with some shithead partner like that after going through the worst thing they'd ever experienced.

"Are you going to tell me what happened?" Cato asked as he parked my car in my spot, and we started to walk toward my apartment, my oversized sunglasses doing little to hide my bruising, and people were looking at me with sympathy, and Cato with suspicion.

He didn't seem to give a shit, though, as he led me into the elevator and then up to my door.

"Yeah," I said, sucking in a deep breath. "But I need ice cream to do it."

Chapter Seventeen

Rynn

"Let's see what he brought," Cato said, opening Eddie's insulated bags on the counter and listing their contents.

"Cheesy scrambled eggs," he started, and I was already doing "gimmie" fingers at him. You couldn't get easier to swallow than soft scrambled eggs. And I needed the protein and the fat from the cheese. "Okay. And... mashed potatoes with homemade gravy," he said. "Then there is some... some sort of soup with those little star pasta. Baked mac & cheese. This is some sort of... cheesy rice, I think," he said as he went to another container.

"How long has he been up cooking?" I asked, feeling a little guilty that he'd spent so much of his time on me.

"Dunno. But he loves doing this, so stop looking all worried," Cato said.

"Have something," I said as I forced down my first bite of eggs. It wasn't the most pleasant feeling, swallowing solid food, but it wasn't as bad as I was expecting either, especially after the throat spray.

"He made me some of everything that's here," Cato admitted, taking out his own eggs.

"This is good," I said, pointing my fork at the eggs. We finished eating mostly in silence as I had to keep washing down the eggs with a cold drink to ease the soreness.

Then Cato brushed me off to relax while he put the rest of the food away for later, coming back with the ice cream I requested to tell this story.

"So you know how I told you my mom is a psycho and my dad was always absent?" I started after Cato thawed my ice cream while I did a quick whore's bath and changed into a fresh tee and panties. I tried to put shorts on, but got frustrated with the bandages and just went without.

"Yeah."

"Well, I did have someone else in my life growing up." Albeit not for as long as I would have liked.

"Yeah? Grandparent?" he asked.

"Uncle," I corrected. "He was older than my mom and absent a lot of my young childhood because he was… stationed overseas."

"Stationed. In the military?"

"Actually, ah, the CIA."

"Your uncle was a spy?" he asked, catching on quick.

That wasn't exactly something I knew right away.

All I knew at first was that he was coming back to Miami, and that my mom was actually cleaning the house and cooking a meal to have him over.

And since I spent most of my childhood eating peanut butter and jelly sandwiches as my dinner and junk food for the rest of my meals, this was a pretty big deal for me.

If I really gave it thought, I could probably only pinpoint half a dozen times my mother had cooked over the course of my childhood. And most of those times were because she was having one of her many boyfriends over for dinner, trying to impress them, make them believe she would be a great wife to them someday.

I didn't get to eat at the table during those meals, of course, but there were leftovers that I could heat up to eat after she and her boyfriend of the week were locked in my mom's room.

So, yeah, the fact that my mom was actually standing in the kitchen all day, slicing and dicing and frying and baking, it felt like a huge deal. Like someone really important was coming to dinner.

The weird thing was, she never really even talked about my uncle much. When I, a curious kid wondering why our family was so small, would ask about her relatives, she would mention she had a brother, but hadn't seen him in years.

At the time, I figured maybe he was in a home like my grandparents were. We'd visited them occasionally, my mom chain-smoking in the car on the way there, her body taut and fidgety.

It was clear that the relationships she had with her parents were... strained. All they did was bicker when they visited, though they'd been nice to me, handing me sugar-free candy out of their nightstands, and telling how pretty and smart I was. Even though they couldn't have possibly known if I was smart since I'd never spent any time with them.

"No, stupid," my mom had said when I mentioned that, rolling her eyes at me. "He's not old enough to be in a nursing home."

Which was not something I understood yet at eight years old. But I filed that information away.

I was ushered into my room when the buzzer announced that my uncle had arrived. I thought that was where I'd be forced to stay, my belly grumbling, my ear pressed to the door, shamelessly eavesdropping.

But the third thing my uncle said when he came in, after greeting my mom, and telling her the food smelled great, was inquiring about me.

"Where's the little ankle-biter?" he'd asked.

My mom sighed, then called out my name.

"Oh, look at you. Haven't been biting ankles in a while, huh?" he'd asked, nodding at me.

My uncle was a tall, thin man. No beard, no tattoos. Dark brown hair cut in a very plain style. Eyes a mix of green and brown I would later learn to call 'hazel.'

Everything about him was… nondescript. You couldn't pick him out of a crowd.

I would be told later that he'd done that by design.

He'd been kind of quiet over that dinner while my mom badgered him about where he'd been, what he'd done, how envious she was that he had nothing tying him down.

I was young, but I was well aware that *I* was what was tying her down.

During that visit, she'd mentioned the apartment building having a few vacancies, but he'd said nothing about it.

Until we found out a week or so later that he'd moved in without a word.

"He's not the brother I used to know," my mother

had complained, shaking her head as we watched him carry his things in the building from our apartment window.

That seemed to be my mother's way of writing the man off. I don't recall her ever inviting him over again after that. And she definitely didn't want to visit his place.

I, on the other hand, found myself completely fascinated by my uncle. Part of that was likely because he was the only other family I had, and I was desperately seeking some sort of connection with someone, since my mom and I weren't close.

I watched his comings and goings, curious why he was always checking his surroundings, always seeming suspicious and anxious.

Eventually, though, he seemed to stop going out at all. Someone from the local grocery store started bringing him his food each week.

That was what actually sent me down to his apartment for the first time.

My mom had been out with her girlfriends for several days in a row during my summer break, and there was nothing at all left to eat in the apartment. And lord knew my mom never let me have any money.

So, at nine, with a grumbling stomach, I made my way out of the apartment, and up the elevator to his floor.

Mid-building. I would later learn that he refused to stay in an apartment or a hotel on a lower or upper level. He preferred rooms with no views, close to the stairwell, and far from the elevators.

"Whatever it is, leave it at the door," a voice had called from inside when I knocked.

"Uncle Chuck?" I'd called back.

There was shuffling, the sound of what seemed like a dozen locks disengaging, then the door was swinging open.

"Munchkin," he'd said, nodding at me. "What're you doing here?"

"We're out of food." I was blunt, even as a kid. Likely because my mom didn't give me a whole helluva lot of time to explain my wants and needs, so I learned not to beat around the bush about anything.

To that, his brows raised. "Where's your mom?" he'd asked, inviting me in.

"I don't know. She goes out a lot."

He sighed at that, but nodded. Then made me an omelet while I poked around his apartment.

"It was full of carefully concealed weapons," I told Cato.

A wall of "decorative" knives on display. A bat here. Tools tucked behind garbage cans or under cabinets. If you needed to defend yourself, you wouldn't be more than a foot away from some sort of weapon at all times.

"You come here anytime there's no food at home," he'd insisted as I ate like a starving child. "Or when you don't want to be alone," he'd added.

He probably didn't mean for me to be there pretty much daily that summer. But that was what he got. A little nine-year-old nuisance that he had to cook for constantly. Who had a million questions about all the places he'd seen.

"The thing was, I think it meant as much to him as it meant to me," I told Cato. "He had nobody. And it seemed like he'd been lonely for a really long time."

"Can't imagine his line of work allowed for a lot of close friendships. What with his entire identity often being a lie."

"Yeah, exactly."

I think, to an extent, he forgot how to be a normal human being with connections. Little ol' me reminded him how to do that.

Eventually, he realized that I wasn't the typical young kid, that I was obsessed with dark themes, that I would always pick a thriller or horror movie over something geared toward my age group.

Then he would slip up, little by little, while we watched those movies, telling me all the ways that the plots or action or fight scenes were inaccurate. Sometimes, we would even recreate the scenes to show me how it *was* possible to bring about the desired result.

And, of course, I was a curious kid.

How did he know all of that?

Where did he learn it?

Could he teach me?

That was when he told me—carefully, of course— about his previous job.

"Secrets, munchkin, are a universal currency."

"That always stuck with me," I admitted to Cato.

"It's a fucking good line," Cato agreed.

"I didn't understand him at first, of course."

It wasn't until he taught me to start observing people, watching him the way he saw them, that it started to click for me.

The neighbor across the hall suddenly started working out, dressing better, and got a stylish haircut. Why would he do that, munchkin?

I would come up with several theories until he taught me to hone in on the fact that people did things for very, very basic, universal reasons.

Love.

Money.

Power.

Revenge.

"Changing his appearance won't give him any money," he'd insisted. "It could give him power, but not in his line of work. And the only person who changing his appearance would get revenge on is an ex. He's married."

Then it clicked.

He was cheating on his wife.

Sure enough, as I started to watch him more myself, even without my uncle, I saw the signs. The way he would stay out late, then come home, spraying himself in his car with his cologne. How he would take a walk to the corner store to call the girl where his wife wouldn't overhear.

I took that information and applied it to life. To school. To classmates.

Everyone, it seemed to me, had secrets.

And if you learned how to use them to your advantage, you could get anything you wanted.

"That was how you came up with the idea to blackmail your father."

"Yeah. I was a master at small manipulations by

then. I even managed to fuck over my mom here and there. Much to my delight. That makes me sound like a bitch..."

"Your ma didn't even make sure there was enough food for you in the house before she took off, leaving you alone, baby. I think she had whatever you did to her coming."

It was nothing big.

Just petty things.

Little ways of getting her back when she had done little but fuck me over and blame me for everything my entire life.

"What about your uncle?" Cato asked.

"Little by little over the years, his paranoia got to him. Fucked with his head. Which led to drugs and then, a while later, a fatal overdose."

"Fuck, Rynn. I'm sorry."

Luckily, mercifully, I hadn't been the one to find him. He'd just so happened to have maintenance scheduled the day after he overdosed. They found him, called the police, told my mom, who then told me.

"Your uncle is dead."

That was all she'd said.

Like the man hadn't been my only father figure. My only *parent* for years.

"Turns out he wasn't just paranoid, though," I told Cato.

"What do you mean?"

"The day after he died, a small crew of men went into his apartment, tossing the entire place, and coming back with some sort of file folder."

Who knew whose secrets were in there.

I wish he'd told me about it.

I would have gotten rid of it for him.

Or, maybe, all that was in there was blackmail to keep the bad guys from getting too close. And once he was gone, it no longer mattered anymore.

"So, you… use what he taught you?" Cato asked, circling me back to the point.

"Yes. After blackmailing my father with his own secrets, I saw all the ways secrets could make me money. Over time, I built up a name for myself. Then I opened my *consulting* business."

"Who hires you?"

"Anyone who wants to find out secrets about other people. Spouses who want to see if their partner is fucking around. Businessmen who want dirt on rivals. And, increasingly, less than… reputable organizations who want something to use against other such types of organizations."

"What percentage of your clients are criminals?" I asked.

"I'd say it is close to fifty-fifty. The night we met, that was not a criminal. I mean, he's probably a criminal," I relented. "In the white collar sort of way."

"And the night this happened?" he asked, reaching out to stroke a finger gently down my bruised cheek.

"Yeah, that was criminals," I admitted. "On both sides," I added.

"What was the job?"

"Recording a conversation that was happening that evening," I told him. "To do that, I needed to break into a loading dock, then a sealed-off room, and finally haul my ass up into the air ducts to climb through to listen through the vents."

"That explains your arms and legs," he said, glancing down at the wraps.

"Yeah. The person I talked to about the ducts assured me that they would hold me, that they would be tight, and that it would be hard to get back out, but he'd failed to mention how sharp everything would have been. Not that I could have worn pants to protect me anyway."

"Why not?"

"Because the place I needed to sneak into was attached to a rave-style club that only let pretty girls in party dresses in."

"A normal club?" he asked, brows pinching.

"A... less than legal club."

If Cato was from the area, he knew that those things weren't common, but they existed. People were always looking for new ways to party. In venues where they could get away with more shit.

Sex clubs.

Dance halls where they could snort and shoot and do whatever they wanted without getting kicked out.

They usually didn't last long once the cops got wind of them.

I couldn't help but wonder if the white supremacist club moved around when the cops closed in. Was that why I needed to crawl through ductwork instead of him finding a way to plant a bug?

"Owned by what kind of criminals?" Cato asked.

"Well, they run the club, but they also deal meth. It's owned by neo-Nazis."

A snarling sound escaped Cato at that.

"Yeah, I know. I'm still furious I had to pay them money to get into that club," I said, shaking my head.

"How did it go wrong?" Cato asked, giving my thigh an encouraging squeeze.

"I still don't know. Maybe there were cameras I didn't see..." I admitted. I'd been racking my brain trying to figure it out, but kept coming up blank.

"Duct sensors," Cato said.

"What?" I asked, brows pinching.

"Some places that have issues with raccoons and shit like that getting into the ductwork, or if they're paranoid of people doing what you did, they can put sensors in the ductwork. Silent alarms or heat sensors. Something that would let them know something or someone was in the ducts."

Which would prompt someone to go and check. But if they'd been dealing with some sort of infestation, they wouldn't exactly worry about bringing backup just to check things out.

I'd been unexpected.

And so, so fucking lucky that it had just been the one guy.

I tended to be pretty confident most of the time. But I wasn't too proud to admit that I didn't stand a chance against more than one of those bastards. That was why I always made sure to be careful, to plan and plot, to find all the possible screw-ups in my plan.

Duct sensors hadn't even been on my radar.

Now, though, it would be something I thought about on every future job I did.

"I had just gotten out of the ducts, bleeding all over

myself, and thought I was home free," I told Cato, knowing he wanted those kinds of details. And finding I actually wanted to share them.

"But you weren't," Cato said.

"A hand grabbed me by the throat and slammed me against the wall," I told him, wincing at the memory even as the adrenaline surge I'd felt then rose within me once more as I relived it. The way my skin felt like it was buzzing, my heart hammering, my legs seeming shaky and weak.

"Then… then there was some punching," I told him, waving at my face. "But I had a bracelet chain that I used to push against his throat, startling him enough to release me.

"But then I ended up on the ground, and that was where shit was going to get a lot worse," I told him. "I had a small knife in my heel, though, and I managed to get that out, and stab it into his face. Then I took that chance to run like hell out of there."

"Did they chase you?"

"Yeah. But I was moving in warp speed, I swear. I tossed my wig, got to my car, and flew out of there. I drove around, then got back to the office to wash all the cover-up off my tattoos, clean myself up, and then head home. I had a splitting migraine, so I took a pill to try to sleep it off. That was when you showed up. And… that's it," I said, shrugging.

"Are you playing it off like that as a defense mechanism, or do jobs go this sideways often enough that you're immune to it?" Cato asked.

"I have close calls sometimes. Like when I had to use you for a quick getaway. But a job has never gone this wrong before."

"Why didn't you tell Josie?" Cato asked.

"Because she worries so much. If she saw this," I said, waving at my face, "she would be a complete mess every single time I went out on a job."

"Why didn't you tell me?" he asked, voice so quiet that I barely heard it. And I was sitting right next to him.

I took a deep breath before turning to face him.

"I'm not used to having someone to share this kind of thing with," I told him. "I've never had someone waiting on my call, or expecting me to show up, or worrying about me when I don't answer."

"Did you think I wasn't waiting or worrying?" he asked.

"I... I don't know," I admitted.

"I called. And texted."

"I never turned my ringer back on after the job. And I didn't expect you to call like that."

"Can I make something pretty fucking clear right now?" he asked, tone still casual, but there was something serious in his pretty eyes.

"Yeah," I said, voice tight, some part of me terrified he was going to tell me that I was a dick for not telling him what happened, that he had no tolerance for chicks who made him wait and worry, that he was done with me.

"I'm in," he said. "In this. In us. I'm all in. The only reason I wasn't making that clearer was because I got the feeling that you might spook if I pushed too hard too fast. But it has pretty much been nothing but you up here," he said, tapping his temple, "since you jumped on the back of my bike."

"You're right," I said, trying to pretend that the gooey lava cake sensation wasn't overtaking me again. "I would have spooked," I clarified, giving him a little smile. "I'm… really bad with emotions and touchy-feely shit like that. I never really understood relationships before."

"But now?" he prompted.

"Now… I don't know. I like being with you, that's all I know. And your friends. And I don't like the idea of you not being around."

"Hey, I'll take it," he said, shooting me a smile I was learning to like way too much. "Then, if or when you want to give me more, I'll take that too," he said, bopping the side of his head into the side of mine.

He couldn't possibly know how much it meant to me that he was willing to give me time. I knew me. I was going to have moments where I needed take time to process things before I could wrap my head around them, then move forward.

"Are you fucking anyone else?" I blurted out, watching as he jerked back at the bluntness before a smile tugged at his lips.

"No, baby. Just told you it's been nothing but you since I saw you that first night. You?" he asked.

"No. And, ah, I… uhm… I don't want to," I said, inspecting my nail bed because this felt like a big deal to discuss.

"Good. I don't either," he said. There was a long pause, both of us lost in our own thoughts. "Think this means we're officially in a relationship," he said finally.

"I… yeah," I agreed, nodding. Was a part of me rebelling against that? Sure. But it was a knee-jerk reaction, something based on past experiences, not the present situation.

"Think I'm kinda happy with that," he said.

"Me too," I agreed.

"Never fucking thought I'd say that."

"Me either," I said, feeling a small smile tug at my lips. "I always thought I would end up rich and single with half a dozen sugar babies around to make me margaritas and rub my feet."

"Well," he said, reaching down to carefully pull my feet into his lap. "You can still be rich. And I can make you margaritas," he said, starting to sink his thumb right into that achy bit in the arch of my foot. "And rub your feet," he said as a mewling sound escaped me.

"Careful," I warned. "I will take advantage of you now that I know this is an option."

"Baby, if there is one thing I will never complain about, it's you taking advantage of me," he said, eyes twinkling.

"Don't look at me like that when I'm too injured to do anything about it," I demanded, pouting.

"Who said you needed to do anything?" he asked, working steadily on my feet.

It was meant to be relaxing.

But there was no denying that he was getting me all hot and bothered just with a foot rub. It didn't help that he was just sitting there, looking so thoroughly fuckable after admitting his feelings for me and spending the past day taking care of me.

I never would have anticipated that someone taking care of me would be such an aphrodisiac, but there was no denying it was the case with Cato.

I guess I had never been open to the potential for anything soft and sweet with the opposite sex being exciting. But Cato and I had fucked hard and rough and had explored slow and sweet. I loved them both.

Cato's magic fingers finished my feet, then he got to his feet suddenly, breaking the spell I'd been under.

"Where are you going?" I asked, trying not to sound as disappointed as I felt.

"Nowhere," he said, leaning over me, reaching out, and starting to draw my panties down my legs, masterfully avoiding the bandages in the process.

Then he was lowering himself down, reaching to spread my thighs wide for him, then sliding between.

His lips pressed to the inside of my knee, then blazing an unhurried path upward, then down the other thigh. Until I was trembling with the need.

Still, he seemed content to torture me forever.

Until my hands sank into his hair at the back of his head and pulled him against me.

His tongue circled the hood around my clit, refusing to give me the direct contact I was aching for until my thighs were shaking and my hips were writhing up into him. Until I was whimpering his name.

Then and only then, his tongue glided across my clit, making a low moan escape me.

It didn't take much for him to start driving me up, making me lose the bad memories, and the evidence of the experience etched into my skin, the pain associated with it all.

All there was for a few blissful moments was his tongue working magic, his fingers sliding inside of me, and the orgasm that screamed through my system, leaving me shaky and exhausted afterward.

He looked up at me after, grinning, pleased with himself, then stole my melty ice cream off the end table and finished it off himself.

"So... what now?" I asked a while later.

I wasn't even sure what I was asking.

What movie next? What were we eating for dinner from Eddie's feast he'd dropped over? What was going to happen a day, week, month from now?

"Now... whatever we want."

That was his answer.

And it was perfect.

Chapter Eighteen

Cato

Rynn managed to be a model patient for all of...
three days.

She let me clean and dress her wounds, bring her
food, feed her cats, do some basic chore shit around
her place.

Sometime in there, we got word from Ama that her
labs were back and there was nothing to worry about.

But by the fourth day?

She was surly and antsy, grumbling when I tried to
do anything for her.

"I can make my own coffee!"

Me? I took that shit with a grain of salt. Because I
knew full-well just how fucking miserable I'd been
after I'd gotten shot, and needed to take it easy, relying
on my brothers to bring me shit, and help me do basic
life tasks.

I was used to being busy, to doing what I wanted
when I wanted to.

It had been beyond frustrating to be waited on and
treated like I was incapable of doing things that used
to come so easily.

On that fourth day, it was fine for her legs and
arms to go without dressing or ointment anymore.
Her stomach wasn't making her wince unless she

bumped it by accident.

Really, she was back to normal, save for the bruises. I had just gotten used to taking care of it. What's more, I enjoyed it.

But it was clear she was done being treated with kid gloves.

"What're your plans today?" she asked when she came out of the shower, her long hair still wrapped up in a towel, and another one around her body.

I had managed to keep my desires to myself, despite her closeness that seemed to immediately overwhelm my system.

I had not kept my hands to myself, though.

Because when she got mopey or frustrated, I found that my mouth and my fingers put her back into a good mood in no time flat.

"Fuck," I hissed as she got closer to the bed, that damn towel slitting up her thigh with each step.

My cock was straining already, pushing out against the sweatpants Levee had dropped off along with a couple other changes of clothes the night after we'd gone to the clinic to see Ama.

"You," I said as she stopped at the end of the bed, taking a deep breath that had her tits straining against the material of the towel. "You're my plans. For the next hour or so anyway," I told her, watching as her lips twitched as her gaze moved over me.

I didn't bother with a shirt like she often didn't bother with pants, so her eyes roamed over the outlines of my abs before seeing my cock straining the material of my pants.

"Oh yeah?" she asked, and when her gaze moved

back up, to my face, her eyes were heated, her lids heavy.

"Yeah," I said, watching as she reached up to pull the towel off of her head, her long hair spilling over her shoulders. The body towel flicked off next, and my cock twitched just looking at her.

"Well then," she said, lowering herself onto the edge on all fours, and slowly crawling up over me, stopping at my waist as she drew down my pants, freeing my cock, and immediately sucking it into her mouth.

My hips bucked up into her warm, wet, tight lips, going deeper as she started to suck me, her head down, her ass high in the air, giving me a great fucking view as she worked me relentlessly until I gathered her wet hair, and pulled until she released me with a little smirk, knowing how close she had me.

"Get up here," I demanded, pulling as she kept crawling over my body, straddling my waist.

Releasing her hair, my hands drifted over her, teasing over her breasts, working her nipples into hardened buds.

The smell of her was everywhere—coffee and chocolate. My senses were overwhelmed by it, by her.

Rynn arched up slightly, reaching between us to slide my cock down her cleft.

She paused, looking at me, seeing if there was some objection.

If this was any other woman, there would be.

I didn't fuck women without condoms. You couldn't be too careful.

But this wasn't any random woman. This was *my*

woman now. And we didn't have to worry about any unwanted—as of this point in our lives—visitors since I watched her pop her Pill every morning.

I pressed my hips upward slightly instead, and she lowered herself down on me with a deep sigh, like she'd been waiting for this forever.

"Wow," she said after a moment, smile big enough to show her damn dimples. "This is better than I expected," she admitted as she started to move.

A first for both of us then.

And I had to whole-fucking-heartedly agree.

I got to really *feel* her this way. The warmth and wetness along with the tightness as she rode me, slow at first, savoring the new sensations, then harder and faster as her body begged for release.

I let her come, her pussy squeezing my cock over and over, before I moved, settling her on her back as I leaned on the edge of the bed and started fucking her, hardly letting her recover from one orgasm before I was driving her up toward another one.

She was even faster than usual, the days of closeness without getting me inside of her like we both knew she really wanted making her crash into another orgasm as I resisted the urge to come with her.

I grabbed her again, turning her over, and pulling her hips back toward me, then surging back inside of her as my hand grabbed a hold of her hair, and my other landed slaps to her ass that had her moaning and slamming back into me in no time.

This time, when she came, I came with her, hissing out her name.

"Okay," she said, energized while I was completely

spent, popping up on her elbow to look over at me where I'd collapsed beside her on the bed. "So, what are you doing today now that you've done me?" she asked, smile playful.

"Eating. Working out. Then doing you again," I told her, getting a little laugh out of her. "You?"

"I have to go into the office for a bit. See what Josie has been up to. Scan and destroy this case file. The usual after a job is done."

"How about we meet back here after?" I suggested. "Then head over to the clubhouse?"

"I have been missing Eddie's cooking," she said, putting a hand on her stomach. "It's a deal. Five? No, six," she decided.

"Works for me." It gave me time to go back to the club and talk to Huck. Since, apparently, I had a bone to pick with the local white supremacists. I mean, you know, other than the bone I already had to pick with a hate group, that is. She shifted, and I got another whiff of that smell of her. "What is that?" I asked.

"What is what?"

"That smell you always have?" I asked, sucking in a deep breath.

"You mean my delicious chocolate coffee signature scent?" she asked, beaming at me.

"Yeah, that."

"I found a company that matches all their scents, so not only does your soap and lotion smell the same, but so does your shaving cream and your hair products."

"Fucking buy stock in that company," I demanded as she shot me a smile as she got up, walking toward the bathroom with her thighs pressed tightly together.

I liked that more than I should have.

Coming inside of her.

It felt almost possessive in a way.

Maybe especially so because it was new for both of us.

She came back out fifteen minutes later in her usual black tank, a pair of black shorts and her combat boots. But she'd carefully applied makeup to cover up the scars on her face. I couldn't even see a shadow.

"Convincing, right?" she asked, turning her head side to side as I looked at her.

"That shit is magic." I mean, sure, the bruises weren't the same shade they'd been the day after she'd been hit, but she'd acquired some yellow and green to go with the fading purple and blue.

"I know, right? This way, when we are walking out of the apartment, people won't stink-eye you, thinking you're beating on me," she said, going to her nightstand to slip a chain bracelet on.

She never used to wear that. But after she gave me the details of the attack, it was clear she now believed she had to wear it 'just in case' shit happened again.

Whether she would admit it yet, to herself or anyone else, that job had changed her. I couldn't help but wonder if there would be other changes, new fears and anxieties, different precautions or paranoia.

Time would tell.

And I would be there to make sure nothing like this shit ever happened again.

"Okay, well, I'll see—" she started as she stood beside her car door.

She lost the rest of that sentence as my lips crashed

down on hers, kissing her fucking silly right there on the busy street. So deep and so long that she looked a little dazed when I finally pulled away.

"I'll see you back here in a few hours," I said, then waited for her to get in her car, lock the doors, and drive off.

Did I wait a bit then drive past her work to make sure she made it there?

Yep.

Then I took my overprotective ass back to Golden Glades.

"How she doing?" Huck asked, already waiting for me, knowing this talk was coming. He'd been through this more than a few times in the past. Each time one of the women somehow got involved in some sort of trouble.

"She's mostly better. Physically, anyway. Time will tell for the mental shit."

"It was bad, huh?"

"She still needed to use this tattoo makeup shit to cover up the bruises. But she got lucky, considering this group."

"Yeahhh," Huck said with a sigh. "That group..."

"I'm assuming you've done some research into them."

"It's not a small organization," Huck said, tone resigned, knowing that wasn't going to stop me from getting some sort of retribution. At the very least to the man who'd put his hands on Rynn.

Did I want to take all the fucks out? Sure. But I also had to understand if Huck could only okay me taking out the one who did the damage to my girl.

"Yeah, I figured. It shouldn't be too hard to find who this guy was. She stabbed him in the face."

"Okay. I can get behind you tracking him down and taking him out. Somewhere rural where you can't be seen or have it traced back to you. I just don't think we have the numbers right now to take on that entire crew. We're working on that, but from what Seeley is saying, they have us three times over. At the very least. I can't risk everyone right now."

"I get that. So long as I can handle this one guy, I'll be satisfied with that. Can I get on that now? Want to find him before his face heals."

"Yeah. We got some extra hands here now, so I can spare you. But be careful. Don't be stupid. I know you get off on the adrenaline, but you got a woman to think of now."

Yeah, that was a first.

I'd rarely considered the consequences of my actions. Because it didn't really impact anyone but me. Sure, Levee and Seeley would be upset if I died, but it was different.

I had a woman to come home to now.

I had a future I was curious to try to build with her.

I had no clue what a life with a woman like Rynn might be, but I was excited to find out.

"I'm just going to… look around for now. I will let you know before I make a move."

"Sounds good. Be smart," he said, slapping me on the shoulder, then moving past me to head back to his own family.

I checked in with Seeley and Levee, each offering to help me, but I brushed them off, figuring I was just going to do some basic surveillance.

With that in mind, I grabbed some food, cold drinks, and an extra large coffee that I stashed in the club SUV that I was borrowing for this task, before heading back out of Golden Glades, and toward the street where Rynn had explained the warehouse was located.

Everything was shut down and inconspicuous in the daylight. If you didn't know better, you would just assume it was one of a few abandoned warehouses in the general area.

I did see a couple of those fucks who ran the club moving in after, I assumed judging by the bags in their hands, had gone out to get lunch.

I was just thinking of heading out to go grab some damn binoculars because I didn't anticipate having to park so far back from the club to not be noticed when, suddenly, about half a dozen black sedans with blackout windows came rushing down the street, parking blocking the entire area off to traffic.

I watched, stomach tensing, as all the doors of those cars opened up, and no fewer than twenty men dressed all in black came out of the cars.

The sun was high in the sky, bouncing off the metal of their guns as they casually circled the building.

The fuck?

What the fuck was I about to be a witness to?

Even as I reached toward the gear shift, ready to back my ass out of there, though, there was a tap on my driver's window.

I saw the gun that had done the tapping first.

Then the man holding it.

A tall, fit, Asian man in another of those all-black outfits.

My hand shot out toward my passenger seat where I had a gun stashed under my bag full of food.

But it was then that I heard another tap.

Another gun.

Another man.

One look in the rearview dashed any hopes that I could just throw it into reverse and floor it the fuck out of this clusterfuck of a situation.

I sat there, not sure what the fuck my next move was, what was going on, and why I was suddenly a part of it.

I heard no gunshots.

But this was a warehouse outfitted as an illegal club. I imagined there was some decent soundproofing going on inside. And I was as far away as I could be while keeping the building in sight.

I sat there, pulse pounding, keeping the guys in my peripheral vision. Which was how I saw when one of them reached for his phone, pulling it to his ear, and listening before tucking it away again.

Then he nodded to his counterparts, and he was tapping the muzzle of his gun on my window once again.

When I looked over, he jerked his head in a way that suggested I open my door.

I didn't really have a choice in the matter.

Maybe I could have tried to shoot it out with these three guys.

But not the five or six others that were already standing outside of the warehouse.

On a sigh, I cut the engine, then opened the door, reminding myself that I had an ankle holster. If I bided my time, I could still try to get out of this.

Take down one of these guys, use their gun, take out more.

It wasn't a great plan.

But it was all I had.

There just wasn't an opening before being led into the building.

Where I found bodies scattered all around, blood blooming through the fabric of their shirts, heads all but exploded with bullets, their limbs landed in odd angles as they died before they even hit the floor.

"Christ," I hissed, looking around.

They were everywhere.

Most didn't even seem like they'd been able to draw their own weapons before they were picked off.

"Go," the guy behind me said, tapping me with the gun, but not keeping it pressed into me.

If they were going to kill me, I figured I'd be dead as all these Neo-Nazis already.

So I followed the guys past all the bodies, down a hall with another set of bodies, and then into an office space.

There, sitting at the desk, eating the food I'd seen the dead guys bring in just a few minutes before, was, it seemed, the leader of this crew.

Whoever this guy was, he was dark-haired, dark-eyed, and clearly spent a fuckuva lot of time in the gym, judging by the way his chest and abdominal muscles were visible through his black tee.

"You," he said, nodding at me as his men backed

out of the room, but stayed right outside the doorway.

"The fuck am I doing here?" I asked, sounding bored and inconvenienced, not worried. Because the longer I was in this building, the less I felt I had a reason to worry.

"That's the question," he agreed, nodding. "I think it must have something to do with the woman who gave me this," he said, reaching into his pocket to reveal a recording device, placing it on the table beside a pile of fries he hadn't touched yet.

"You're Rynn's client," I said, the pieces falling together.

Rynn likely had given him the device while I was heading back to Golden Glades. He'd listened, decided to take action, and just so happened to do so while I was looking for Rynn's attacker.

"Glad to know she didn't share that information," he said. "She came highly recommended.

"She got beat to shit on this job," I said. It wasn't an accusation. But it was close.

"I noticed." My confusion must have shown, because I hadn't seen a hint of bruising under her makeup when she left. "She doesn't wear makeup like that," he said, shrugging. Seemingly unbothered by what had happened to her.

"Who are you?" I asked.

"Jai Xú," he supplied.

It took a second to register before his name finally clicked.

An old story from before mine and Levee's time at the club. Involving Che and Che's girl. Who'd gotten herself mixed up between The Yakuza and The Triad.

Jai Xú was the leader of the latter.

A man who'd shot his own brother in front of Che and Saskia when he'd found out he'd fucked up.

Coldblooded, was one word Che had used to describe him. A man who shot his brother dead, then told Sass and Che to leave, so he could plan his brother's funeral after his "tragic" death from an "brain aneurysm."

"And you are another of those bikers," he said, gaze moving over me.

"Yes. To be fair, Jai, I had no idea this had anything to do with The Triad. I was just here—"

"For revenge," Jai supplied.

"Yeah."

To that, he nodded, grabbing a napkin to wipe his mouth and hands, then standing.

"Come," he demanded, turning his back on me, clearly not worried about me trying to act out.

And, yeah, if this was The Triad, there was no way I was shooting my way out of this situation, even if they wanted to try to kill me.

I followed Jai down a long hallway, past the restrooms, and then into the open space of a loading dock.

Where more of Jai's men were standing there with another man on his knees between them.

One with a nasty hole in his face.

"I figured this was your kill, yes?" Jai asked, waving casually toward him.

"That was what I was here for," I agreed.

"Be my guest," Jai said, shrugging. "Don't worry about the mess," he added, turning and walking away.

"I hear the building is going to suffer a disastrous fire. Such a shame this building was supposed to be abandoned. The sprinkler system just never turned on..."

With that, he was gone.

A moment later, so were his men.

Leaving me alone with the fuckhead who had beaten Rynn, who would have done more, who may have killed her, taken her away from me. If she hadn't been so determined to fight, to get away, to come back to me.

I'd killed before.

I would kill again.

But there has always been something detached about it.

This?

This was personal.

I won't repeat the litany of racist-ass shit this dickhead had to say about Jai and the rest of The Triad.

"Your ass would be here with me with or without The Triad," I said as he finally decided to get up on his feet.

"Don't even fucking know you."

"No. But you know my girl. You put your hands on my girl."

"Fucking sluts, y'know?" he said, shrugging and shaking his head.

"No, asshole," I growled. "You beat the shit out of my girl," I told him, tossing my bike cut toward the side, hoping not to get any evidence on it.

I saw the realization dawn on him just a second

before my fist collided with his face.

He was a big guy.

We were well-matched in a fight.

And, normally, his will to live should have given him an advantage.

But in this case, it was my fucking rage that won out.

I was only partially present in the fight.

I was mostly imagining Rynn's beautiful, battered face, the look of fear in her eyes when I first woke her up, the way she winced when she moved or tried to talk.

But I was also in this warehouse, seeing Rynn trying to rush out, only to have a grown-ass man grab her, choke her, and punch his fist into her face over and over.

I did the same, knuckles hitting the bastard's granite jaw, his nose, his eye, his stomach, ribs, then, finally, spleen.

The pain doubled him over, making him drop down to his knees.

I didn't give him mercy.

He wouldn't have given it to Rynn.

I kicked him hard in the side, sending him flying.

Then I dropped down on him, knee on chest, then pressing my hands around his throat like he had done to Rynn.

His body thrashed.

His eyes bulged.

But then, slowly, he went limp.

I didn't let go.

Limp didn't mean dead.

In the end, he was a bloodied pulp, and my knuckles were aching as I rose up to the sound of slow, deliberate applause.

And there was Jai Xú.

"Very eye-for-an-eye of you," he said as I approached my cut, and slipped it back on. When I looked again, he had a cigarette between his lips, and was holding an ornate silver lighter flicked open in his hand as a few of his men moved into the room carrying something in little red and yellow bottles.

Accelerant, I had to imagine.

They sprayed a healthy amount over the man whose name I didn't know, didn't care to know, that I'd just killed.

"You should get going," Jai said as his men rushed out of the room, and Jai casually walked closer to the body, took a long drag of his cigarette, then dropped it down on the man's body.

The flames were almost instantaneous.

Big and angry.

But Jai just stood there, watching them lap at the body for long enough that I debated going over there and grabbing him and pulling him away.

Eventually, though, he took a step back, turned, and walked out of the room.

I followed, smelling more accelerant in the main area of the warehouse, noxious enough to make me hold my breath as I walked through, then out the door where I sucked in some fresh air before making a beeline for my car.

I didn't say anything else to Jai or his men.

I figured my business with them was done.

I didn't drive all the way back to the club, choosing instead to drop in on Teddy to let me wash up there.

"Cato," Teddy greeted me as I walked into his penthouse.

Now, sure, Rynn had a penthouse.

But there was a difference in Rynn's kind of money and Teddy's kind of money. The "old money" sort. Coffers so deep that it would be borderline impossible to spend all that money in his lifetime.

Rynn's living, dining, kitchen, and guest room could probably fit into Teddy's living room.

The kitchen was off to the side, everything industrial and fine quality.

His penthouse was much like the man himself. Effortlessly classy.

I wasn't sure I'd ever seen Teddy not completely put together. He had a suit collection—vests, pocket squares, ties or bowties, and cufflinks included—that made it so I rarely saw him in the same one twice.

He had a cream one on this time with a slightly darker, patterned vest beneath.

He didn't, for once, have one of his many hats on.

"This is a pleasant surprise," he said, keen-eyed gaze taking in the way I was flexing my knuckles, and the bruise that had to be forming on my jaw from where the bastard got one good punch in. The rip in my shirt where he'd yanked at it. "You know where the bathroom is. There should be a change of clothes in there that would fit you."

"Thanks, Teddy," I said, going into one of his guests rooms to get cleaned up, taking my shirt out into the hall to drop it down the trash shoot before making my way back in, finding him already waiting there with a glass of whiskey in his hand for me.

"Just you?" he asked.

"It was… personal," I told him, tipping back my drink. "My girl was roughed up on a job," I explained.

"Your girl?" he asked, brows raising. "That's news to me."

"It's new but going somewhere."

"Good for you," Teddy said, nodding. "I can't tell you how irritating it is to watch your brothers fight their growing interest in women they are clearly meant to be with."

Teddy had always been a voice of reason in the relationships that built in the clubs. He was also the kick in the ass some of the guys needed to make them realize they had fallen in love, and they needed to hold onto that.

I had no idea what had happened in Teddy's life to make him romantic that way, but it was an interesting dynamic to have around.

"So what is she like?" he asked just as my phone started to ring in my pocket.

"Sorry," I said, seeing Rynn's name on the screen.

"Ah, what the fuck, Cato?" she snapped, loud enough that Teddy's brows lifted even standing several feet away.

"What the fuck what?" I asked, brows pinching.

"The news, Cato," she snapped.

"News?" I asked Teddy, who nodded, then grabbed this giant-ass tablet that ran his whole apartment, and flicked on the framed TV.

There it was.

The fire.

Raging.

"Oh, that. That, believe it or not, wasn't me. That was a new friend of yours," I explained, hearing a long silence on the other end of the phone.

"Oh," she said. "Okay. Well… where are you?" she asked.

"Invite her over," Teddy said. "We can go to eat," he added.

I rattled off Teddy's address, telling her I was with a friend if she was interested in grabbing something to eat with us.

This was Rynn we were talking about.

She didn't turn down food.

And she liked all of my friends so far.

Not twenty minutes later, I buzzed her up, then waited for her at the door.

Her gaze went right to that bruise on my jaw.

"I mean, I'm not *innocent*," I told her. "But I didn't set any fires," I added, leading her inside. "Teddy," I said as I closed the door. "This is…"

"Rynn," Teddy said, head jerking back at the sight of her standing in his living room.

"No fucking way," Rynn said, smile spreading until I saw one of her dimples.

"You two know each other?" I asked, looking between them, confused. It wasn't like Teddy and Rynn would run in the same circles.

It was Teddy who spoke.

"I've hired Rynn for more than a few jobs," Teddy informed me.

"Secrets are valuable in business dealings," Rynn

said, nodding. "I can't believe you guys know each other…"

"Our world is an English village," Teddy agreed. "How about we go out to eat, and I can explain how I became involved with a bunch of bikers," Teddy said, putting down his glass, then grabbing his suit jacket, and walking toward the door. "It involves grand theft auto."

"Our meet-cute involved forcing someone into being a wheelman against their will," Rynn said as the three of us moved into the elevator.

Later, after Rynn had taken her car back to her place, I was standing with Teddy on the street next to my SUV.

"That's your future wife right there," he said, nodding sagely.

And when you had Teddy's stamp of approval, well, you knew you found the one.

Even if I had no fucking idea what a happily ever after would look like with a woman like Rynn.

I guess I was about to find out.

Epilogue

I waited on bated breath, some part of me terrified that the fires would in some way trace back to Cato or me.

Me, because of my connection with Jai Xú. I was the reason Jai had the information to go after the white supremacists to begin with.

I wasn't worried, of course, that the blood I'd spilled in that warehouse might trace back to me. From the footage I'd seen on the news, the place was practically ash.

I had no idea what the hell Jai and his men had used as an accelerant, but it was really fucking effective, that was for sure.

Of course, no amount of fire could completely erase the fact that bodies were found in the wreckage.

Dental records even came up with names. Though no one was grieving the loss of members of a hate group.

There was no surveillance on the street. I knew that because I'd scoped it out myself. The best the cops could come up with was grainy footage of black cars driving down the road before and after.

The problem being that the plates were fake and the windows heavily tinted.

Jai Xú was nothing if not very good at what he did.

Organized crime was all over. And while it wasn't rare to hear of the Italian or Irish mafia, even the Bratva getting accused of crimes, I don't think I had ever heard of The Triad being brought in on anything.

Knowing Jai, the guns that had been used for the fire were untraceable and long since gotten rid of.

Nothing would trace back to him.

But I didn't have the gory details about the whole thing with Cato. So I was terrified something might trace back to him.

Because of me.

I wasn't stupid.

I knew he'd tracked down and killed that man for me.

Jameson Cutter.

His name had been on the news. A rap sheet as long as my arm with a string of warrants for unpaid child support to four kids from three different moms.

No one was mourning the man's death. Least of all me. But I would feel like I was to blame somehow if Cato got in trouble for being the one to end his miserable life.

But when the news leaked that Cutter hadn't been shot, I breathed a sigh of relief. If Cato had killed him some other way, the evidence was long gone. Cutter had been identified through dental records because he'd been so burned.

It was over.

Maybe I should have felt weird about the killing. But, I mean, I knew what I was getting into with Cato. His club wasn't the weekend warrior sort. They were one-percenters. They did illegal shit for a living. And that illegal shit, undoubtedly, meant there were feuds with enemies that ended in bloodshed occasionally.

I mean... Cato had been shot in the stomach.

Any illusions I had about his job not being dangerous disappeared the first time I saw that scar.

The thing was, it didn't bother me.

My feelings would be entirely different if I knew that innocents were getting hurt. But this was strictly business shit. *You fuck with us, we fuck with you.*

Besides, I was no saint.

I believed down to my bones that I was capable of killing someone in the right situation. I actually think most people are.

So there was no reason for me to go around like I was the morality police when I knew I was capable of the same thing.

Besides, in a dark and twisted sort of way, I was flattered. He'd tracked down the man who'd hurt me, and he'd made him pay.

"Rynn," Josie called, snapping me out of my swirling thoughts.

Reaching for the remote, I turned off the office TV.

"What's up?" I asked, giving her a smile.

"I asked how things with Cato are going," she said, hearts all in her eyes.

"They're... good."

"Why the hesitation?"

"I'm not used to all of this," I admitted, shrugging. "I don't know what to say."

"I mean, you're spending every spare minute together," she said.

That was true.

Some nights, he drove out to Miami. Others, I went to Golden Glades.

"We do. It's nice. It's kinda two different worlds, there and here."

When I was at the clubhouse, we spent a big chunk of our time around his club brothers. I wasn't complaining. I loved them. Even the crazy-ass new guy, Coast. And the standoffish, quiet lumberjack named York. Velle, he was harder to decide what my feelings were regarding him.

I mean, he was very nice.

Very easy to talk to.

Too easy to talk to.

Within thirty minutes of sitting next to him by the pool, I was suddenly confessing all sorts of personal shit about my nonexistent relationship with my mom. And I just... I didn't do that kind of thing.

It was almost unsettling how easy he was to talk to.

Hence the not knowing how to feel about him.

"But when you're in Miami?" Josie prompted after I babbled for a long time about the club.

"It's like we're playing house," I told her.

It was interesting how easily we fell into a comfortable rhythm. Picking places to order from, eating while watching one of my action or horror movies.

While I fed the cats, he would take out the trash and wash up any dishes we used.

We'd brush our teeth side-by-side.

If I was sweeping the main space, I would find him cleaning the bathroom.

It was all just so... easy.

"I don't understand," Josie said. "Do you want it to be hard?"

"I think I just assumed it would be."

"I mean, to be fair, this is kinda the honeymoon stage, right? I think the harder stuff comes when things need to be negotiated and decided on. When someone doesn't get one hundred percent of what they want."

"That's fair. We haven't really done a lot of talk about the future. But it's still really new."

"But you are thinking about the future?" she asked, trying to hold back a smile.

"Yeah."

"With him?"

"Yes," I admitted, the first time I'd really done so aloud.

"Like... white dress and baby booties kind of future?"

"Josie, come on. Get real. It would be a *black* dress," I said.

"And would your baby live like that goth baby I see all over social media?" she teased.

"I mean, if it lives with me, it won't have much of a choice."

"Have you informed Cato that he has to dress up with you for Halloween yet?" she asked.

"No, I haven't told him that yet," I admitted.

"Told me what?" Cato asked, making us both look over to find him standing there with a tray of coffees.

"That you'll be forced to dress for Halloween if you want to stay with Rynn," Josie said, accepting her iced latte with a smile.

"Is that right?" he asked, brows quirked as he looked at me.

"Yep. And I will also drag you to every haunted house, haunted hayride, haunted woods, basically anything with Halloween vibes in a hundred mile radius."

"Sometimes, she is one of the serial killers in the haunted woods," Josie piped in.

"You ever scare the pee out of a bunch of cocky teenagers? It's a blast," I said.

"So what am I dressing up as?" Cato asked.

That was something you just had to love about the man. He just kind of... went with the flow.

"You should do a couples costume!" Josie said, beaming.

And, bless her for bringing it up. Because, obviously, that had been all I'd been thinking of. I'd never had someone to do a couples costume with.

"What's a good couples costume?" Cato asked.

That answer was really simple.

"Gomez and Morticia."

Cato - 3 months

I thought she'd been exaggerating about the Halloween thing.

She... had not been.

And since she didn't really have an outdoor space to decorate, she'd decided to go hard at the clubhouse.

"No one's gonna see it all the way out here," Levee said as he helped her drag the dismembered body of a giant skeleton toward the center of the yard. "This isn't a very busy road."

"Um... we'll see it," she said, rolling her eyes at him, refusing to let him dull her enthusiasm. "Besides, Huck's and Che's kids live here. Everyone else's kids visit here. They will see it. I hope they're made of tough stuff, because I'm going to make this spooky as fuck," she declared as I hefted what had to be the twentieth bag of decorations out of her car.

There were lights and gravestones, fog machines and cobwebs.

And, apparently, there would be several deliveries over the next few days of life-sized animatronics meant to scare the bejesus out of anyone who walked past and triggered their motion sensors.

None of this included what she'd already been working on inside.

The staircase had an interesting new garland running up it. Made of different shaped knives with bloody edges, jars with various "preserved" body parts, hands that poked out of the wall, eyeballs hanging from the light fixtures, bloody handprints and police tape on the windows, and doll heads used as planters and candy bowls.

She'd confessed to me the night before that she'd always loved Halloween growing up, but her mother hated everything about it to the point where she refused to even buy Rynn a costume to wear, leaving her the only kid not dressed for the parades the schools put on.

So, clearly, the way she went overboard was a way of healing that sad, inner child who was never allowed to indulge in the things she loved.

"All this effort, we should be having a Halloween party," Levee said, always looking for a reason to party.

I could see by the way that Rynn perked up that there was going to be no way of denying her that.

"Should invite the Ruthless Knights over," Levee said. "We said we wanted to do it, but haven't gotten around to it."

"You could run it by Huck the next time you see him," I said, shrugging.

He really was interested in having them as allies. And what better way to have someone over but for a legit holiday sort of party.

Decorations, food, candy, girls, drinks.

The usual shit.

"Eddie and I would have a blast figuring out a Halloween-themed menu," Rynn said, already seeming like she had a dozen ideas.

"Can't make 'em dress up, though," Levee said. "But I'd be into the club girls showing up in 'slutty kitty' or 'sexy tiger' costumes..."

"Naughty Nurse has always been a favorite of mine," Coast said with a smirk as he handed a tibia to Rynn.

"It is a classic for a reason," Rynn agreed. Though she much preferred costumes that had more of an effort put into them. She was having her damn Morticia floor-length black dress specially made to fit her like a glove. And, apparently, my Gomez suit too.

Josie informed me that there might be outfits for the cats as well. I'll admit, I was going to get popcorn to sit back and watch her try to put anything on that hellcat Binx.

"Maybe I should invite Josie to the party," Rynn mused to herself out loud as she connected a leg bone to a hip bone. "These things should come assembled. I'm not a fucking doctor," she grumbled.

"Who's Josie?" Coast asked, interest piqued.

"No one you will ever put your manwhore hands on," Rynn shot back. "Unless you want your balls to end up in a preservation jar on display for next Halloween.

Rynn told me that she actually had this hope that Josie and the neighbor dude she had some sort of complicated relationship with—the details of which she would not tell me, citing 'girl code'—might work things out.

Which was an oddly romantic sentiment for Rynn.

But, then again, this was a woman who could wax poetic about how amazing Gomez and Morticia's relationship was. So maybe it was wrong to think she wasn't romantic, just that she had never seen herself finding that sort of relationship.

"Ugh, damnit. Is Ama here?" she asked. "Ama!" she yelled before anyone could answer her.

A moment later, Ama herself walked out of the front step, holding a pumpkin coffee cup in her hands.

"What's up?" she asked as Seeley walked out behind her, pressing a kiss to her hair as he did so.

"We need an anatomy lesson here," Rynn called out. "What is this?" she asked, lifting up a random body part.

Ama made her way out onto the lawn, instructing Rynn, Levee, and Coast as Seeley and I watched on.

"You gotta lock that down," Seeley said, drinking Ama's coffee as Rynn used one of the skeleton's enormous hands to whack Levee on the back of the neck with.

"I plan to," I agreed. "Seems like I have to let her get through spooky season first, though."

There was no rush.

I was enjoying the fuck out of every step of this journey.

"Okay, so, tomorrow," Rynn said several hours later, leaning against my shoulder, completely fucking beat.

They'd gotten a good head start going. It was going to be fucking epic when all the shit arrived to finish it up.

"Let me guess," I said, leaning my head onto hers. "You have something Halloween-themed planned."

"Well, I mostly just need pumpkins. Like an

inordinate amount of pumpkins. Like whatever you are thinking, multiply it by ten."

"That's... a lot of pumpkins," I said, nodding.

"We won't be able to get them *all* in one day. But we can get started tomorrow. Oh! And gourds. I always loved those stupid, pimply things. My uncle would order one for me with his groceries every year, and I would keep it with me until it started to cave in on itself and mold. Then my mom would toss it away. But I want those."

"Let me guess. Ten times what I am thinking," I said, smiling because it was impossible not to get caught up in her enthusiasm for the season.

"Maybe fifteen."

"I wonder if Teddy has a pick-up truck in his fleet..."

Cato - 1 year

I had a ring in one pocket and keys in another.
It was a big fucking day.
Full of changes.

The good kind.

The kind we'd been working toward for a year now, tripping toward forever on graceless feet because it was new to both of us.

"Um… yeah, I'm still not exercising for you," Rynn declared, arms crossed, squinting down at the kayak.

"Baby, like I would ever expect you to," I said, waving the one paddle at her. "Get your pretty ass in," I demanded.

This shit had been in the works for months now.

I always knew I was going to propose on the dock where we'd had our first official date. But I'd been pleasantly surprised to find something out about said dock while I'd been making my plans.

"If an alligator is looking particularly hungry today, I will be sacrificing you to save myself," Rynn warned.

"I am well aware," I said with a smile, only more and more sure about these decisions with each passing moment as we made a familiar path through the water toward a dock where we were going to have lunch. And make the forever kinds of plans.

"What are you waiting for?" she asked when I tied up the kayak. "Get up there and pull me up like last time."

She was completely clueless.

I'd been worried when I'd suggested another kayak ride, she would immediately suspect what I had in mind.

Luckily, this was one instance where her lack of romantic fancies worked in my favor.

She probably just thought I only had one good

romantic date idea, and was reusing it almost to the day of the last time we'd been here.

"Listen," she said when I lifted her up. With the fucking cooler in her hand. "I love you. And I want to do you," she added, making my lips twitch up. "But I'm starving, so it has to be after I eat."

And, well, I knew from experience never to get between Rynn and her food.

So we ate sandwiches prepared by Eddie. We drank beers and watched the water as a duck with a black head, silver body, and white wings flittered around in the water while occasionally letting out a quack that went unanswered for a long time before his mate finally appeared, rushing down the bank, and swam into the water.

It was quiet.

Peaceful.

And her belly was full.

So it was perfect.

The next time she looked over at me, I had the box in my hand and the lid popped open, showing her the black diamond nestled in some ornate-ass setting that looked straight out of a gothic movie.

"No fucking way," she said, mouth falling open. But in a good way. "I love it," she said, reaching for it. "I mean, I love you too, but I really, really love it," she said, making my lips curve up, unsure if she actually knew what was going on here or not.

"Baby, I'm supposed to be asking you something here," I told her.

"Well, duh," she said, already slipping it on her ring finger. "And I'm answering," she said once the ring was on, so she could wiggle her fingers at me. "Come on. Grand romantic speeches just so isn't us," she said, reaching out to grab me by the front of the shirt, and pulling me on top of her as she moved flat on the dock.

Then we did something that *was* very us.

Fucking on a dock over the water, oblivious to if anyone was passing by and seeing it all go down.

It was only after, bodies spent, curled up with each other, that I remember this was a two-part surprise.

And my pants with the keys had been casually tossed to the side in my eagerness to get inside of her.

"Shit," I hissed, turning away, then getting up to go grab my pants, careful not to upturn them.

Thankfully, I could feel the outline of the keys inside.

"What?" she asked, not bothering to cover up, just looking over at me in all her naked glory.

"I have something to show you," I told her.

"Think you're showing me everything right now," she said, her gaze moving over me.

"Come on, get dressed," I demanded as I got back into my own clothes. "Or come naked, but there are probably cottonmouths around here," I warned.

That got her up and moving, throwing her clothes back on and making sure her combat boots were on tight.

"Where are we going?" she asked as we followed the narrower part of the dock toward the shore, then onto the ground.

"This is the part where I am going to make you do some exercise," I informed her, surprised how dense the vegetation had gotten just in the few weeks since I'd been here last.

She grumbled and moved to walk behind me.

"What are you doing? There's enough room to walk by my side," I said, waving to the empty space.

"I'm staying right here," she said, placing her hands on my shoulders. "I'm using you as a human shield in case of a snake encounter."

"Of course you are," I said, unable to stop the smile on my lips as I led her up the overgrown path.

"Ah... not that I am morally against trespassing, since we just fuck on these peoples' dock and all, but this seems like it is someone's house," she said as it came into view.

It was a little rundown from outside. And, admittedly, inside too.

The bank had owned it since before I'd brought her here the first time, and it looked like it had been neglected for at least that long.

"It is," I agreed, reaching in my pocket, then turning with the keys held up. "It's ours," I told her, watching as she went from confused to shocked then, finally, as a smile spread across that gorgeous fucking face.

"No way," she said, rushing toward me, and snatching the keys from my hand.

"It's a little rough..." I acknowledged as we walked up through the backyard.

There was an enclosure around the kidney-shaped pool that looked like it needed some repair. And the pool itself would likely need to be drained, repaired, and refilled.

But, hey, it was there. The potential for something awesome was within reach.

"That's the best part," Rynn declared, practically skipping toward the house, going around the front. "It looks like people were murdered here. Were people murdered here?"

"I, ah, I didn't ask," I admitted. "It was vacant for a long time, though."

"Well, we can pretend it was a murder scene, and that the unhappy spirits still haunt the halls..."

"Whatever knocks your socks off, baby," I agreed, following her as we rounded the front of the house.

It was a mess.

Everything was overgrown and covered in moss thanks to the thick canopy of trees overhead keeping it shaded and the ever-present humidity keeping it damp.

The house itself was a sprawling ranch.

Not as grand, structure-wise, as Rynn's penthouse, but a big, solid house that could withstand a beating that the storms sometimes battered us with.

It needed a good power wash, a new front step, and shutters that weren't a hideous red, but again, the potential was there.

And Rynn loved decorating.

Stabbing the key in the locks, she pushed the door open, revealing ancient tile floors with dark grout, a large living room, a dated kitchen, and a dining room to the other side.

Off the kitchen toward the back was a family room. And down off the living room was a hall that led to three bedrooms.

More than enough.

Even if we did have a kid or kids. We hadn't really discussed that yet. But we would be prepared when we decided on that.

"It's rough..." I said as I followed her into the kitchen.

"That's the best part. We can make it completely our own. I have so many ideas already," she said, grabbing my hand and pulling me with her back through the living room, then into each of the bedrooms and bathrooms.

"You're going to have to get real cool about dark paint colors really fast," she told me when she was done checking out every room.

"Baby, anything you want to do with it," I said, waving around the space, "you just tell the prospects, and they will have it handled."

"It's so fun to have workers at our beck and call. I should feel guilty about making them do all the heavy lifting around here..."

"They'll like a break from washing the bikes and cutting the lawn," I said, shrugging it off.

Paying your dues was something we all had to do. Especially when you are at the club and eating the food and enjoying the drinks and girls, but not trusted enough yet to actually do the work of the club. So you had to make yourself useful.

"The cats are going to love the catio."

"Catio?" I asked.

"The pool enclosure," she said. "Obviously, that is going to be their catio."

"Of course it is," I agreed, smiling.

"Is this done? It's yours?"

"Ours, yes," I said, nodding. "It turned out being perfect. There is the sentimental value of it," I said. "But it was also a steal since it's been sitting so long. And it's close enough to the clubhouse that Huck was cool with it."

There was one beat before she just... launched herself at me.

"I am so excited," she said, hanging on as I spun her around twice. "For the house. And the future," she clarified.

And, fuck, so was I.

Whatever it held for us.

Rynn - 2.5 years

"I say this with all the love in the world I have for

you," Josie said as she handed me my tube of lipstick I'd picked out just for this occasion. "But I never thought this was going to happen."

She looked stupid pretty in a deep red gothic-style gown that really brought out her pretty skin and the red highlights in her strawberry blonde hair.

"Well, to be fair, this has been in the works for like a year now. If I'm going to do this, though, it had to be during Halloween."

I mean, who *didn't* want a Halloween wedding?

Beach weddings had been done a bajillion times over. But a spooky wedding shoot amongst red, yellow, and orange foliage in a pumpkin patch, maybe with a hidden serial killer hiding in the shadows? Now that was original.

Sure, it meant I had to have a damn *destination* wedding. Albeit just to New England. But I didn't care. This was what I wanted. And Cato was happy to oblige me.

I loved the man, but he didn't know a damn thing about themes and decor. So he was glad to leave it up to me to throw together. With a helping hand from Josie, who seemed to live for this shit. And, unexpectedly, Teddy. Who knew more about New England than the rest of us, and was all-too happy to have us all flown up privately, and stay in his family estate.

Yes, he used those words.

Family estate.

If that wasn't the most old-money shit you'd ever heard.

It *was* an estate, too.

Thirty-something acres. And it was all *fenced.* Wrought iron fencing. The expensive shit.

I mean, I made good money.

I didn't make thirty acres of wrought iron fencing money. And that wasn't even counting the enormous gates that opened with a little buzzer.

It had twelve bedrooms. Fifteen bathrooms. A conservatory, a steam room, theatre, tennis courts, an indoor *and* an outdoor pool, and a pool house that had two bedrooms, its own kitchen, and the biggest soaking tub I'd ever seen.

Josie and I were currently situated in the guest house where Cato and I were staying. Everyone else was crashing in the big house.

We hadn't *all* come.

Huck hadn't been comfortable leaving just the new prospects at the club with all of us so far away. Besides, he and Che had a ton of kids between them, so they'd decided to hang back. Remy and his girl had as well, on account of all their animals, and the club animals. They also offered to cat-sit for us. And McCoy, because he was so dedicated to the club, decided to stay home as well.

But we had a lot of the crew with us.

Seeley, Ama, and Levee, of course.

Eddie, that went without saying.

Coast had come, but Velle and York had decided to stay back.

Donovan, his wife, and his wife's sister had tagged along for the fun. So had Alaric.

And, of course, I had Josie.

Who was still oddly concerned about my black

264

gown, even though I'd been clear from the beginning I wasn't going to do a white one.

"Who would believe that *I'm* virginal?" I asked, shaking my head.

It was going to be a long-ass day.

The wedding was being held outdoors on some amazing part of the grounds that Teddy had picked out.

Then we were going to do photos here, then at a pumpkin patch and apple orchard while the caterers and such set up.

Then it was eating and drinking and partying the night away.

And hopefully, if we weren't too exhausted or wasted, consummating our marriage in the swanky guest house.

We were staying an extra two days before all heading back home. Just in time for Halloween.

I'd tried to talk Cato into a Beetlejuice and Lydia theme, but he wasn't feeling all the makeup. That also meant Joker and Harley were out too. Jack and Sally were also a no-go. For now. I was going to ease him into those more advanced couples costumes.

He was going to be a serial killer. And I was the slutty cheerleader who had to be killed because she wasn't good and virginal like the final girl. Very specific of us, but it would do.

The clubhouse was practically a tourist attraction now. Something I knew Huck wasn't a huge fan of.

Which was why I was going to need to sit Cato down for a serious conversation about more storage for Halloween supplies at our house, so I could go crazy with decorations each year.

I'd been going crazy decorating for ages.

Josie called it "nesting."

But that sounded too much like something you did when you were about to have a little baby in said nest. And I wasn't. We weren't. I was still popping my little Pill every morning.

Though, yeah, we had both been open to the idea of a kid.

Kid.

Singular.

Neither of us wanted a whole football team of them like some of the other guys were going for.

"You look amazing," Josie decided when I finished with my lipstick and got to my feet.

"So do you," I said, looking at us both reflected in the mirror.

She and Ama were my bridesmaids.

Cato had Seeley and Levee as his groomsmen.

It was a small bridal party.

But it suited us.

"Ready to do this?" she asked.

Amazingly, as someone who never saw herself married and 'settling down,' I was. Because it was Cato. Because there was no one else in the world I'd rather spend forever with.

"Absolutely," I agreed, taking my bouquet of red roses, and following her out.

Cato - 4 years

"I feel like this is a bad omen," Rynn said, shaking her head in an exaggerated sadness.

She looked really fucking amazing for having spent the past sixteen hours trying to get our baby out of her body.

"That's it," she had said down to her belly as the nurse rolled her wheelchair up toward the maternity ward, "This is your eviction notice, dude. Like I love you and all, but I want you the hell out."

She'd had a very up and down pregnancy.

From almost the moment the stick gave us the news, she'd could be found almost constantly with her head over the bowl.

She couldn't eat anything down until eventually even the thought of food made her sick.

And this was Rynn.

Food was one of the most important things in her life.

So, yeah, you can imagine she was miserable for the first four months.

She lost weight. She got thin. She could be found staring daggers at me in a very 'You did this to me' sort of way.

But the second trimester had given her a reprieve. She stopped getting sick. Her appetite came back. Doubled. Tripled. Fucking quadrupled. She was so ravenous that even Eddie struggled to keep her full.

That was the honeymoon period.

She nested, decorating the nursery with an almost obsessive focus. She bought clothes and strollers and dragged me to the dealership to pick out a 'safe but not completely hideous' family car.

Oh, but then… then she got really, really pregnant. Which brought on acute back and shoulder aches and charley horses that kept her from sleeping at night. Her feet and ankles swelled, making wearing shoes almost impossible, and walking of any sort painful, so she pretty much spent the past three weeks with her legs propped up, eating ice cream, and telling the baby that it was lucky she loved it because she was miserable.

"What's a bad omen?" I asked, turning back from the window with our baby in my arms.

"Oh, come on," Rynn said, rolling her eyes. "What day is it right now?" she asked.

Then it dawned on me.

She'd gone into labor on Christmas Eve.

Which meant the baby's birthday was on Christmas day.

"Listen, if you wanted a spooky baby, you should have jumped me in February instead of April," I told her.

"I jump you constantly," she shot back, making a nurse who'd come in to bring another blanket that Rynn had requested laugh. "It's your swimmer's fault for being especially motivated that day," she said, shaking her head. "I guess I have to learn to be as into Christmas as I am into Halloween," she declared. "Why are you keeping my baby from me?" she asked. "I'm the one with stitches in her hoo-ha. I get all the baby snuggles."

I moved over, lowering the arm of the bed, and climbing in with her, moving the baby into her arms.

"She's perfect," Rynn decided as she looked down at her.

She came out a chubby eight-and-a-half pounds, full of rolls and a shocking amount of dark hair.

"She is," I agreed. "Takes after her mother," I added.

"She better. I did all the hard work," she said, leaning her head into me. "Though I wouldn't mind if she got your pretty eyes. And maybe your patience. Lord knows I am lacking in that particular quality."

"We will have to let her Uncle Eddie teach her how to cook, since neither of us are any good at that," I said.

"And her Aunt Josie will teach her how to fall in love with books," Rynn agreed. "Uh-oh. She's squirmy again," she added, shifting our daughter slightly so that she could expose her breast. "Hey, at least she gave me big tits for all the headaches she caused in utero," she said before guiding the baby to nurse.

"One of the many good things she's going to bring to us, I'm sure," I agreed, unable to stop myself from reaching out and stroking my finger down her impossibly soft skin.

"Oh! I figured it out!" Rynn said, eyes round.

"What?"

"Our first family Halloween costume," she declared.

"Oh, yeah? What's that?"

"You get to be Wesley. I'll be Princess Buttercup. In the red dress, not the blue. And she can be an R.O.U.S!"

"The fuck is a R.O.U.S?" I asked.

"A Rodent of Unusual Size," she said, rolling her eyes at me.

"You want our baby daughter to be a rat?" I asked, laughing.

"Oh, she won't even know what she is. We have to do the fun stuff before she's old enough to decide it's not cool to do family Halloween costumes anymore."

"Can't argue with that," I agreed.

"You'll make the cutest giant rat, won't you, Aggie?" she asked.

Aggie.

Short for Agatha.

A character from *Halloweentown* that I'd never seen until Rynn made me sit down and do so.

We'd gone through all sorts of names. From the more macabre—Samara, Blair, Carrie—to the niche and odd—Buffy, Sally, Bella(trix)—and finally, the slightly more tame, but still Halloween-themed—Agatha, Piper, Winnie.

But Agatha, and in particular the shortened version of Aggie, had won out.

Rynn had decided to give her a Christmas-themed middle name too.

Agatha Noel.

I knew the both of us couldn't fucking wait to see how she was going to turn out.

Rynn - 18 years

"That," I said, walking down the dock toward where Cato was sitting off the edge of it, watching Aggie paddle around the water, "is no child of mine. Willingly exercising? The horror," I said, dropping down next to Cato who automatically wrapped an arm around me.

"I would worry she'd been swapped at the hospital if it weren't for her inhuman ability to put away white cheddar popcorn just like her mother," Cato agreed.

"This is true. White cheddar popcorn cravings are more accurate than any paternity test," I declared, watching as Aggie suddenly started paddling in a circle.

Too fast.

Too reckless.

Too much like both of her parents.

"Damnit!" she cried, almost falling over the side of the kayak to retrieve the book that she'd sent flying over into the water in the process.

Yep.

We were the kinds of parents who let our fourteen-year-old curse.

And recklessly twist her kayak around in alligator-infested waters.

"There's a healthy dose of her Aunt Josie in there too," Cato decided, as Aggie desperately tried to dry the sopping book with the very shirt she was wearing.

She looked like us.

Tall and slender, but the slightest bit bottom-heavy like her mom. With long, dark hair, but really gorgeous green eyes like her father.

She was, at times, the best and worst of us.

Stubborn and thrill-seeking.

But kind-hearted, loving, and confident.

I think, through raising Aggie, Cato and I had managed to heal a lot of the wounds from our own childhoods.

Where we may have endured endless birthdays with no cakes or presents, we showered our girl with extravagance and surrounded her with love.

Where I hadn't been allowed to dress up for Halloween or go pumpkin picking, we all dressed and took yearly trips to New England to really get the fall vibes.

Through her little girl wonder, I had even learned to fall in love with the wonder of Christmas. Which had meant that Cato needed to put an extra storage shed on our property to accommodate all of the decorations I had accumulated over the years.

She got all of the love and security that we hadn't gotten, which had allowed her to grow up just slightly more open, more trusting, and less cynical about the world.

We watched as Aggie paddled back to the dock, and climbed up the ladder.

"Can I call Aunt Josie to see if she'll take me to the bookstore?" she asked, showing us the damaged book. "It was just getting good."

"I'm sure she'll be happy for an excuse to go to the bookstore for the fourth time this week," I said, nodding. "You know where my wallet is," I added.

Aggie had unlimited book-buying money.

I'd mostly stepped back from the secrets-dealing business over the years, wanting to spend more time with my family, and less time potentially getting myself hurt or killed. But I'd lucked out in finding several other people who still had that thirst for adrenaline and espionage as I once did. They mostly did the jobs now. While I got to just collect a portion of the income.

Which left me time to devote to my true passion. Golden Glades only Halloween village.

Sure, it only operated for three weeks out of the year, but it took me all year to make it bigger and better each time.

I was even considering creating off-shoots of it in

other states in the future.

Eventually.

For now, I was content.

A couple minutes later, Aggie was yelling from the backyard, telling her that Aunt Josie was there, and they were going book shopping, then getting lunch.

"I mean, for old time's sake," I said when I was sure she was gone, climbing onto Cato's lap.

There was never any hesitation with him.

His lips were on mine, and his hands were sneaking up under my shirt, teasing over my skin, then drawing it up and off, tossing it carelessly behind us.

He leaned me back on his legs then, making my head hang over, the water below me, the sky above, and Cato leaning over my chest to tease his lips over my skin.

It was always like this with him.

Even after these years.

Shivers and anticipation.

Losing track of time and surroundings.

Getting completely lost in each other.

That warm, gooey lava cake sensation afterward.

All these years later.

"You know what we need right now?" I asked.

"Lava cake?" he asked, knowing me so damn well, already reaching for his phone to get it ordered.

"And something horrifically gory on the TV."

Aggie did turn out to love Halloween.

But she didn't like the really bloody shit that I did.

"With a little foot massage to finish things off with?" he asked, reaching down to help me to my feet.

"See, I knew there was a reason I married you…"

If you liked this book, check out these other series and titles in the NAVESINK BANK UNIVERSE:

The Navesink Bank Henchmen MC
Reign

Cash

Wolf

Repo

Duke

Renny

Lazarus

Pagan

Cyrus

Edison

Reeve

Sugar

The Fall of V

Adler

Roderick

Virgin

Roan

Camden

West

Colson

Henchmen MC Next Gen
Niro

Malcolm

Fallon

Rowe

Cary

Valen

Cato

Dezi

Voss

Seth

The Savages
Monster

Killer

Savior

Mallick Brothers
For A Good Time, Call

Shane

Ryan

Mark

Eli

Charlie & Helen: Back to the Beginning

Investigators
367 Days

14 Weeks

4 Months

432 Hours

Dark
Dark Mysteries

Dark Secrets

Dark Horse

Professionals
The Fixer

The Ghost

The Messenger
The General
The Babysitter
The Middle Man
The Negotiator
The Client
The Cleaner
The Executioner

Rivers Brothers
Lift You Up
Lock You Down
Pull You In

Grassi Family
The Woman at the Docks
The Women in the Scope
The Woman in the Wrong Place
The Woman from the Past
The Woman in Harm's Way

Golden Glades Henchmen MC
Huck
Che
McCoy
Remy
Seeley
Donovan
Cato

Shady Valley Henchmen MC
Judge
Crow

Cato

Slash
Sway

STANDALONES WITHIN NAVESINK BANK:
Vigilante
Grudge Match
The Rise of Ferryn
Counterfeit Love
Of Snakes and Men

OTHER SERIES AND STANDALONES:

Stars Landing
What The Heart Needs
What The Heart Wants
What The Heart Finds
What The Heart Knows
The Stars Landing Deviant
What The Heart Learns

Surrogate
The Sex Surrogate
Dr. Chase Hudson

The Green Series
Into the Green
Escape from the Green

Seven Sins MC
The Sacrifice
The Healer
The Thrall

The Demonslayer
The Professor

Costa Family
The Woman in the Trunk
The Woman in the Back Room
The Woman with the Scar
The Woman on the Exam Table
The Woman with the Flowers
The Woman with the Secret

DEBT
Dissent
Stuffed: A Thanksgiving Romance
Unwrapped
Peace, Love, & Macarons
A Navesink Bank Christmas
Don't Come
Fix It Up
N.Y.E.
faire l'amour
Revenge
There Better Be Pie
Ugly Sweater Weather
I Like Being Watched
The Woman with the Ring
Love and Other Nightmares
Love in the Time of Zombies
Primal

Under the pen name JGALA:
The Heir Apparent

Cato

The Winter Queen

Jessica Gadziala is the USA TODAY Bestselling author of over 100 steamy romance novels featuring all sorts of twisty and turny plots, strong heroines, lovable side characters, steam, and epic HEAs.

She lives in New Jersey with her parrots, dogs, rabbits, chickens, ducks, and her bearded dragon named Ravioli.

A big thank you to Fern for always putting such care and attention into helping these books be the best they can be.

And also a thanks to Ashley, Sonya, and Cherie for helping make this book shine.

Connect with Jessica:

Facebook:
https://www.facebook.com/JessicaGadziala/
Facebook Group:
https://www.facebook.com/groups/314540025563403/

Goodreads:
https://www.goodreads.com/author/show/13800950.Jessica_Gadziala

Twitter: @JessicaGadziala

Website (and newsletter): JessicaGadziala.com

Amazon:
https://amzn.to/3Cwa5ei

TikTok:
JessicaGadziala

Discord:
https://discord.gg/yXCvuWTJ

Spotify (for book playlists)
https://open.spotify.com/user/jessiegadz?si=f636a0e5e19b4b1a

<3/ Jessica

Made in United States
Cleveland, OH
22 March 2025

15430994R00166